Journey Through Llandor is the first in Louise Lawrence's compelling trilogy. The fantastic world she creates is seen through the eyes of Carrie, Roderick and Craig, teenagers who are unsuspectingly lured into the world of Llandor, Irriyan and Mordican by the evil Grimthane.

Louise Lawrence lives in Gloucestershire in a house she and her husband spent two years renovating. She has three grown up children.

She says of her writing: "I never have been responsible for what I write – only responsible for the way I write it. Inside my head is a cinema screen. On it, at times never of my choosing, I watch the whole story being played out from beginning to end – plot, characters, names, faces, landscape, conversations – everything. My job is to remember what I see and write it down to the best of my ability."

The Llandor Trilogy
by Louise Lawrence

Journey Through Llandor
The Road to Irriyan
The Parting of the Ways

JOURNEY THROUGH LANDOR

LOUISE LAWRENCE

Collins

An Imprint of HarperCollins *Publishers*

First published in Great Britain by Collins in 1995
Collins is an imprint of HarperCollins*Publishers* Ltd,
77-85 Fulham Palace Road, Hammersmith,
London W6 8JB

1 3 5 7 9 8 6 4 2

ISBN 0 00 675022 2

Printed and bound in Great Britain by
HarperCollins Manufacturing, Glasgow

for Ann-Janine

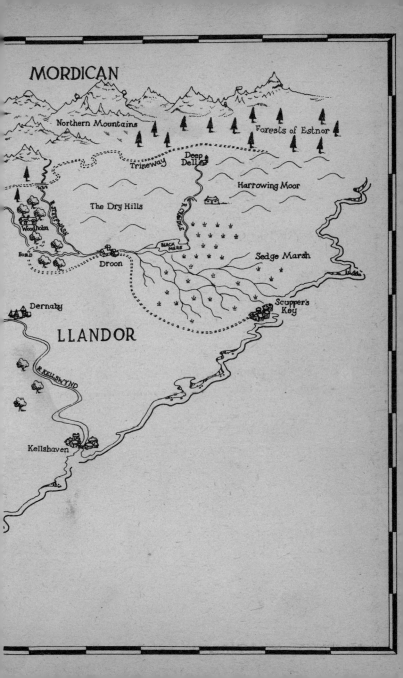

CHAPTER ONE

As the bus from Lydminster approached the turning to Ditchford, Roderick picked up his school bag and rose from his seat. Then someone pushed him, a hand in the small of his back that sent him hurtling forward. He knocked into Carrie, who knocked into Craig. Bags and books scattered beneath the seats, and Roderick clutched at the handrail to save himself falling.

Craig elbowed him in the gut. "Look where you're going, Fatso!"

"You great clumsy oaf!" hissed Carrie.

"It wasn't my fault!" whined Roderick. He hauled himself upright, and a biro snapped beneath his foot.

"Now look what you've done!" yelled Carrie.

"I couldn't help it, could I?"

"That was my best biro!"

"Someone pushed me!" said Roderick.

Carrie bent to pick up the pieces and Craig retrieved their books from beneath the seat. As Roderick squeezed past them the bus stopped with a jolt, flinging him backwards.

"You're treading on my hand!" howled Craig.

"Sorry," said Roderick.

Craig's voice was venomous. "You'll be sorry, all right, when we get off this bus!"

Everyone was laughing – students in navy blue blazers giggling and sniggering wherever Roderick looked, their eyes bright with enjoyment. They wanted Craig to hurt him, wanted him to beat him up. He hurried down the aisle towards the exit as Craig and Carrie searched the floor for a lost history book.

"Hurry up!" the driver shouted impatiently.

Roderick alighted into late afternoon. Autumn sunlight shone over the fields that flanked the main road, and the hedges were scarlet with hips and hawthorn berries. But the walk home up the nearby lane offered him no pleasure – only pain, if Craig and Carrie caught him. He knew he could not outrun them, but beyond the fields was a small wood with chestnut trees, a short cut past the vicarage that might provide somewhere to hide.

Hastily Roderick climbed the stile and headed along a footpath through the cow pasture, seeing his shadow stretching before him, and the church tower showing above the trees ahead. The bag of school books banged against his legs as he ran. When he crossed the stile into the wood Craig and Carrie were already close behind him.

He gained the sanctuary of the trees, his footsteps loud among chestnut husks and the mounds of dead leaves. Then the other two were in the wood, the sound of their pursuit growing nearer and nearer. He could already smell his own sweat. It ran down his face and soaked his shirt, and his breathing hurt – hard gasps that failed to fill his lungs with air. And the same fear drove him that had driven him throughout his life, fear of what they would do to him, the hurt to his body and the anguish of his own emotions, the kind of torment he had endured before, over and over, but had never learnt to bear.

Desperately he turned from the path, blundered towards a holly thicket beneath the larger trees, dark leaves shining with light that offered a chance of concealment. Oak twigs tangled his hair and sharp leaves scratched him as he forced his way through. And just for a moment he noticed how the dark boughs curved before him, making a perfect arch, a gateway, perhaps, that led into a different world where he could escape for ever. But then the ground gave way beneath him and he went slipping and sliding among brambles and bracken and tree roots, down the slope and into a hollow filled with leaves.

For a while Roderick lay motionless where he had fallen, flat on his back, staring up at a tracery of twigs against the blue autumnal sky. He watched the leaves fall softly, gold and brown, drifting down to join the mass on which he lay. And the scent of earth was all about him, rich and strong, pungent with the season, smelling of leaf-mould and fungi and decay. His heart still hammered from the effort of running, from leftover fear and the narrowness of his escape, but he did not think he was injured. The leaves had cushioned him and the sweet, kind silence of the trees soothed away his fear.

He waited until his breathing eased, then struggled to his feet and brushed the dirt from his clothes. A triangular tear in his new school trousers showed the white flab of his thigh beneath. The contents of his bag were strewn around him. He shook the wood lice from his maths book, retrieved the cover of his English exercise book and the pages torn from a textbook on practical chemistry. He would be in trouble now, he thought dismally, both at school and with his mother.

Unwanted tears filled his eyes. He was always

in trouble of one kind or another, always the butt of other people's jokes and other people's nastiness. He sometimes wished he had never been born, wished he did not have to be himself, Roderick Burden, fat and hopeless, but could be someone else instead. He sniffed despairingly, wiped his eyes on the sleeve of his blazer, picked up his pencil case and stuffed it in his bag, then stared up the slope down which he had fallen.

He thought he was lucky he had not been killed. Great trees grew among outcrops of rock, among clumps of nettles and briars, and saplings with spindly trunks leant against each other for support. His trail showed clearly down the slope between them, earth scrubbed clean by the seat of his trousers, and the dark mass of the holly thicket at the top. He looked for an easier way up. But the hollow was all around him, tumbled rocks and undergrowth, and there was only a single diagonal path leading out of it that went in the wrong direction. Reluctantly, and encumbered by his school bag, Roderick began to climb...until he heard voices.

Craig and Carrie appeared above him.

"Thought you'd lost us, did you?"

"Well, tough luck, Burden!"

"We're coming to get you right now!"

"You stinking fat git!"

"We're going to sell your guts for blubber!"

Roderick slid backwards into the hollow. And they came after him, were halfway down the slope before he hit the ground. Then he was running again, the rolls of his fatness jolting and shaking with every step as he headed along the path. The way seemed endless, grey trees all about him, old and bearded, their gnarled branches reaching like arms as if they were alive and knew he was there. Snaking roots now and then tripped him. And he should have reached the churchyard wall long before now, but the path led on and the trees grew more and more menacing, their silence unbroken by the rasp of his own breathing or the gleeful cries of pursuit from behind...until suddenly Carrie screamed and Roderick stopped.

He held his breath and his heartbeats boomed in his head. And she screamed again, a long-drawn-out wail of terror as Craig howled Roderick's name. They were trying to scare him, he thought, lure him back along the path where they were waiting in ambush. But he was not about to fall for that. His held breath exploded and his lungs pumped like bellows, sucked at the air and refused to be filled. He hardly heard what Craig was shouting. Then finally the words became clear...desperate, imploring.

"Answer me, Burden! For pity's sake! You've got to be there! We're sorry we threatened you! But you can't leave us here, not like this. Please,

Rod! Please!"

Roderick glanced behind. There was no sign of them. Just the empty path curving through the trees.

"What do you want?" he shouted.

"Give us a hand!" yelled Craig.

"Why should I?"

"Quickly! Quickly! The tree's got Carrie!"

"What do you mean?"

"It's alive, I tell you. And it's got Carrie!"

"You must think I'm stupid!"

"You've got to believe me! Please, Rod!"

Something communicated...the use of his proper name, the fear in Craig's voice and Carrie's hysterical weeping. Roderick did not think they were play-acting...and all around the grey trees seemed to be watching. But the impression faded as he walked, slowly, warily, back along the path. The low sun slanting through the branches made the woods briefly beautiful. Leaves glowed with autumn colours and mottled patterns of shade flickered over the undergrowth beneath.

He rounded the bend...saw Carrie on the ground and Craig clinging to her. The red sweaters that identified them as school prefects were unnaturally bright, out of place among the soft gold–brown tones around them. He thought for a moment that Carrie must have fallen and sprained an ankle, until he approached and recognized the truth. A tree root had twined round her leg, a grey snake-like coil that was pulling her down through a crack in the earth. And in the darkness beneath, pale tentacles of other roots reached towards her, blindly searching.

"Get it off me!" she sobbed.

Roderick stared in horror. Then he looked up. There were eyes in the bark, or holes that resembled eyes...the bole of a nose and a crack in the trunk that leered like a mouth...the vague features of a monstrous face staring down at him, bearded with moss. The tree was alive, just as Craig said. And Roderick was paralysed with fear.

"Do something!" begged Craig.

"Please!" wept Carrie.

"Like what?" whimpered Roderick.

"Just give me a hand," groaned Craig.

Roderick swallowed and put down his school bag. Reluctantly, he took one of Carrie's arms, and he and Craig together tried to pull her free. But the tree would not release her. The crack in the earth widened and the pale roots coiled round her other leg and tightened. She screamed and struggled but slowly, inexorably, the tree was pulling her in.

"It's useless!" said Craig. "We need an axe or something."

"I could run to the vicarage," offered Roderick.

"There isn't time."

"I've got a penknife in my bag," Roderick said hopefully.

"Get it," said Craig. "We'll give it a go."

"And please hurry!" wept Carrie.

Roderick tipped out the contents of his school bag, sorted through the mound of books and crisp bags and chocolate wrappings, found the knife and opened its blade. Then, kneeling at the side of the hole, he hacked at the nearest root until the pale sap bled. The tree thrashed wildly above him and other roots reached for his wrists. He pulled back in alarm.

"It's useless," he panted. "I'll never cut through them with this."

"And it's hurting," sobbed Carrie.

"There's matches in my pocket," Craig said grimly.

"You mean burn it?" asked Roderick.

"We've got to try, haven't we?"

"We could set fire to the whole wood!"

"Just do it!" said Craig.

The gold prefect's badge shone on his lapel and it was automatic. Roderick did as he was told, felt in Craig's blazer pocket, found a battered packet of cigarettes and then the matches. If Craig smoked then he was the stupid one, thought Roderick, but he did not say it, just silently gathered an armful of fallen twigs and dry bracken and piled them in a heap at the foot of the tree. It seemed to know what he was doing. It bent and creaked and the branches reached for him, twiggy fingers groping like hands. He ducked beneath them, added more twigs and a few larger sticks as Craig implored him to hurry and Carrie slipped deeper into her tomb beneath the earth.

Finally Roderick tore the pages from his English exercise book, shoved them beneath the pile of kindling, lit a match and stood back to watch. Smoke curled upwards in blue drifts. And the tree grew agitated. Its branches trembled and a look of alarm showed on its face, a flicker of fear in the black pits of its eyes. Then there were little tongues of fire leaping around it, a crackle of flames among the twigs at its feet, and the gap of its mouth opened wider in a silent wail of anguish. And suddenly Roderick was aware of his own power.

"Let Carrie go and I'll put it out," he said.

The tree shuddered.

"I mean it!" he said firmly.

Finally it obeyed. Its leaves sighed, its snaking roots withdrew. Craig pulled Carrie free and the crack in the earth began to close. Satisfied, Roderick dismantled the bonfire and stamped out the flames. There was a patch of blackened bark at the base of the tree, but no real damage. The huge face regarded him, silent and resentful, but he was no longer afraid of it. For the first time in his life he was in control of a situation.

"Don't do it again!" he commanded.

It seemed to bend in acknowledgement. Then the impression of its face faded and it was just a tree, rooted in earth, its gnarled branches hung with moss, its leaves shining yellow in the sunlight...no different from any other tree. And they were all more ancient than any Roderick remembered in the woods round Ditchford. He frowned in puzzlement and turned to the others. Carrie sat on the path, rubbing the weals on her legs. Her face was white as a sheet, streaked with dirt and tears, and Craig was beside her, his face equally ashen.

"Where are we?" Roderick asked.

"Middle Earth?" suggested Craig.

"Where's that?"

"In a book," Carrie said shakily.

"*The Lord of the Rings*," said Craig.

"Ha ha!" said Roderick.

"That was definitely an ent," said Craig.

"What's an ent?"

"A tree person," said Carrie. "But they weren't malignant."

"Old Man Willow was," said Craig.

"This is an oak tree, Craig!"

"But it got you, didn't it?"

"I want to go home," Carrie said tearfully.

"And I want my dinner," said Roderick. For

the second time that afternoon he gathered up the contents of his school bag as Craig helped Carrie to her feet. He was no longer afraid they would beat him up. That fear was gone in another greater fear...fear of what had happened and where they were.

"We must have come through some kind of doorway," said Craig.

"It did look like a doorway," said Roderick.

"What did?" asked Craig.

"The holly thicket," said Roderick.

"And there was a steep bank with a hollow at the bottom," said Carrie. "It should be easy enough to find."

"We only need to retrace our steps," Craig said confidently.

Roderick followed where they led. And the path divided, twisted among the trees, divided again and led steeply downwards. They returned to the burnt oak and began again, several times, but they always took the wrong turning and the path led downwards. The old trees brooded as the sunlight faded. Now and then they caught glimpses of faces that vanished when they stared. White mist drifted towards them up the wooded slopes and darkness gathered behind. The day grew late and cold and still they wandered, searching for the hollow and the holly thicket and a gateway home.

"This is hopeless," said Craig.

"What's happening to us?" whimpered Carrie.

They paused to listen. There was no sound in the woods except the soft falling of leaves and the distant chuckle of a stream, a flutter of wings among the high branches and the hoarse cry of a crow, Roderick heaving for breath and his stomach rumbling with hunger.

"No wood can be this big," he panted. "I mean, we ought to be back in the field by now. And why can't we hear the main road traffic? And I don't remember a stream near Ditchford either...I mean, it's dry, isn't it? Except in wet weather."

"We're not *in* that wood," said Carrie.

"So where are we then?"

"Somewhere else. Some other world."

"I don't understand."

Craig turned on him. "Why have you got to be so flaming thick, Fatso?"

"But it doesn't make sense!" said Roderick.

"Haven't you ever read any fantasy books? Played any computer games? Heroes and Quests, that kind of thing?"

"In my grade we don't have computer studies," said Roderick.

Craig glanced at him scornfully. "Don't you have literacy lessons either?"

"It's not his fault!" muttered Carrie.

"Yes it is!" Craig said angrily. "If it wasn't for

him we wouldn't be here, would we? He was the mindless git who blundered his way in!"

"But we didn't *have* to follow him," said Carrie.

"No," agreed Craig. "But if he led us in here he can flaming well lead us out! Get moving, Fatso! And make it quick! I don't want to spend the night in these woods!"

Reluctantly Roderick led the way. Hunger pains gnawed at his stomach and the darkness deepened. He had no idea where he was, but Craig and Carrie followed him anyway. And once again the path led downwards. Chill mist drifted round him and the chuckle of the stream grew louder, but no one suggested they ought to turn round and go back. Clutching his school bag, Roderick simply continued on his way, his footsteps shuffling through the leaves until finally he led them out of the woods and on to a path by a river. It was pale within the darkness of its valley, its rushing water reflecting the last gleams of daylight, wisps of mist rising from its surface.

"Wrong again," muttered Roderick.

"I don't believe it!" wailed Carrie.

"You great steaming idiot!" shouted Craig.

"What'll we do now?" asked Carrie.

"We'll have to climb back up," Craig said angrily.

"My legs ache," whined Roderick.

"And it's almost too dark to see," said Carrie.

"Have you got any better suggestions?" asked Craig.

"No," said Carrie.

"So let's get going, then!"

"I can't!" groaned Roderick.

"In that case you can stay here," Craig said brutally.

He made as if to leave, then hesitated on the edge of the path. It was almost totally dark beneath the trees. And the woods were full of patterings and rustlings and soft sinister sounds. Then, from high up the slope, came the unmistakable bloodcurdling howl of a wolf...and from along the valley another answered it.

Fear that was worse than hunger gripped Roderick's stomach. And none of them stopped to question. They simply ran, their footsteps pounding along the river bank, not knowing where they were going and no longer caring. The water chuckled, and the white mist shifted and drifted, and the wolves howled in the forests above them. Yet Roderick heard nothing but the labour of his own breathing, the rolls of blubber slapping around his midriff, the blood booming in his ears... the efforts of his body that failed to keep pace. In spite of the wolves, in spite of his fear, he was falling behind, further and further as Craig and Carrie sped on.

He tried to shout, but his voice was feeble and neither of them heard. They vanished into the mist and the darkness and left him alone. Sweating and gasping, Roderick stopped, heaved and vomited and collapsed on the grass at the side of the path. He was fat and unfit and could not go on. And the wolves would find him, tear him to pieces. It was all he was good for now – maybe all he had ever been good for – a snivelling heap of human flesh that no one liked and no one wanted, his only purpose to feed the wolves in some unknown land. Howling and slavering, they came through the trees towards him. And he saw his death in the yellow shine of their eyes.

CHAPTER TWO

"Here, Festy!"

"Here, Jag!"

"Here, Benna!"

"Leave, Lodi! Leave!"

"Come to heel!"

"Good boy!"

"Good girl!"

"Good Festy."

The wolves obeyed. Their tongues lolled, their breath steamed, and their yellow eyes gleamed in the twilight, but they kept their distance. Roderick sat up and surveyed his rescuers, a man, tall and bearded, and a girl no older than himself. They were dressed alike in strange old-fashioned clothes – shirts or tunics made of sacking-like material, trousers bound round their legs with leather thongs and knee-high boots. They wore cloaks, too, but he could not distinguish the colours; some kind of silk, maybe, that shimmered and changed with their movements, reflecting darkness and light.

"Are you hurt?" asked the girl.

Roderick shivered. His sweat had grown icy from cold and sickness, and he was speechless in her presence. To him she was almost magical, her braided hair pale as moonlight and reaching almost to her waist, her voice clear and sweet as the river water and the wolves docile at her feet.

"Perhaps he does not speak our language?" said the man.

"Shall I take him to Mother?" asked the girl.

"Aye," said the man. "Do your best to set him at his ease while I go and round up his friends."

"Some friends," said the girl, "if they abandon him in the face of their own fear!"

The man shrugged.

"They are other-worlders, Janine. Their ways may not be our ways. And you, perhaps, should not be so quick to condemn."

"Friendship is friendship, Father, wherever it exists."

"Well, that's as maybe."

"Had they been wild wolves..."

"Now is not the time for discussion, daughter. I must away after the other two and you must tend to this one. Keep Festy with you for security."

"Why?" asked Janine. "These woods are safe enough."

"So we may think," replied her father. "But the trees whisper and there may be others who listen beside ourselves. Not all creatures are loyal to Llandor, remember? If the Grimthane should hear of their coming..."

"Why should the Fell One care about other-worlders?"

"It depends on their purpose, Janine."

"You think they have been drawn here?"

"Is it not usually so?"

"What use can Llandor have for a trio such as these?"

"I'll leave that to Keera, daughter."

He whistled softly, turned and strode away along the river bank after Craig and Carrie, the wolves loping beside him like grey shadows until, at a gesture of his hand, they bounded ahead. Only Festy remained, crouching in the nearby darkness, fierce eyes fixed on Roderick, watching and waiting. Janine knelt beside him. One slender hand reached to touch him, but he jerked aside, afraid of her powers.

"I won't hurt you," she murmured.

"I already know that," said Roderick.

"So you do speak our language after all!"

"I *am* English," he informed her.

"You have understood what was said between me and my father?"

"Some of it."

Janine smiled and rose from her knees.

"Shall we go then?"

"Where?" Roderick asked suspiciously.

"Home," said Janine.

"To Ditchford?"

"I've never heard of Ditchford," said Janine. "We'll go to Woodholm, it's not far. Unless you prefer to stay supperless and sleep the night in the open?"

"I'd rather not do that," Roderick said hastily.

"Then come with me," said Janine.

It was an invitation he could hardly refuse, not with the woods full of carnivorous trees and ravening wolves, and the temperature plummeting towards zero. Shivering in his thin school blazer, Roderick walked beside her, back along the river bank the way he had come, with Festy following silently behind.

It was freezing already, the mist turning to rime on the rushes by the river, whitening the trees on the slopes above him. And frosty stars were beginning to show – familiar constellations that assured him he was still on the same planet, in the same position in the northern hemisphere where he had always lived. And although the landscape was nothing like the landscape around Ditchford, he was fairly convinced the village could not be far away. But his conviction faded when Janine opened the door.

It was set in a bank of earth beneath the roots of a tree, an oaken door almost concealed by ferns and ivy. Yellow light from an inner passage fell across the path and shone in Festy's eyes. But the wolf made no attempt to enter. It remained on the path, settled on its haunches, and the door closed soundlessly as Roderick followed Janine inside.

He was trapped, then, in an underground passage with no way out. He felt briefly alarmed, his mind on the point of panic, imagining a dungeon in which he might be locked for the rest of his life. But almost immediately the feeling faded, was replaced by a sense of total security – as if, as long as he stayed there, nothing could ever hurt him or harm him or render him miserable again.

"It's Keera you are aware of," said Janine.

"Who's Keera?" asked Roderick.

"My mother," said Janine. "Nothing bad can come within her presence."

"Do you know what I'm thinking?" Roderick asked curiously.

"No," she said. "But sometimes I can feel your feelings. I am my mother's daughter, although not as accomplished as she. Come, I'll take you to meet her."

Tree roots grew through the ceiling above their heads, and the passage opened into a larger hall with doors leading off. Or maybe it was part of the forest itself, an underground glade carpeted with living grass and flowers. And the light seemed brighter, warm and yellow as sunlight coming from no source. Through an archway at the far end Roderick saw a pool of water, flanked by stones and steaming with heat, like a natural bathroom. But he had no chance to explore. Janine opened a nearby door and ushered him inside.

The room was a kitchen. There was a flagstone floor, a rough wooden table with a bench either side, earthenware crocks on wooden shelves and bunches of herbs hanging from the ceiling. And in the centre was a raised fire pit. A conical chimney built on four stone pillars funnelled the smoke upwards through the roof. A blackened kettle steamed and sang on a metal grid above the glowing coals, and a woman in a blue and yellow gown stirred a cook pot.

"Mother?" said Janine.

She turned and smiled, and Roderick gazed at her in awe. Her gown was ankle length, its silken colours merging to green and shimmering with light, and her fair hair was braided and coiled about her ears. He did not know her, yet he felt he had always known her – her smile, her face, the soft blue of her eyes, her gentleness, her strength. She reminded him of his own mother, or how he wished his mother could be, without her frown of disapproval and her whiplash tongue. His own mother would have remarked on the tear in his trousers, the dirt on his clothes, not smiled in welcome as this woman smiled, as if she were glad to see him.

"Do you have a name?" she inquired.

"Roderick," he stammered.

"Roderick," the woman repeated. "And you may call me Keera, although I have many names. But you are cold, Roderick. Put your bag over there by the wall, then bring a stool and warm yourself by the fire. The nights grow chill this autumn season."

He did as she bade, fetched a stool that stood beneath a curtained window, leant his elbows on the wall round the fire-pit and held his hands to the blaze. They were not coals, he noticed, but round glowing stones, and however long the fire burnt it did not consume them. He stared in fascination. And Keera stirred the cooking pot, disturbing a scent of stew that made his stomach churn with longing. Beyond, Janine set the table with bowls and plates and cutlery, baskets of bread and fruit, and woven place mats for six people.

"Are you expecting visitors?" asked Roderick.

"Just Kern and your companions," said Keera.

"I was right then?" said Janine.

"Right about what?" asked Keera.

"I said they were not his friends."

"I don't have any friends," Roderick informed her.

"Yes, you do," said Janine. "*We* are your friends – Mother and me and Father and Festy."

"I mean, where I come from I don't have any friends," said Roderick.

"It must be a very sad place," said Keera.

It was, thought Roderick. It was horrible and lonely, a place where no one liked him, not even his own family. Maybe he was glad to be out of it; no more school, no more bullying from his fellow students, no more sarcastic remarks from the games master about how useless he was, no one to tell him he was thick or force him to do his homework – although he supposed his parents might be worried. They would hardly want him to be missing and presumed dead, even though, secretly, they might be glad to be rid of him.

"May I use your telephone?" he asked.

"What's that?" asked Janine.

"I need to call my mother – tell her I'm all right."

Keera's kind eyes regarded him.

"Your call will not reach her, I fear. Although

she will know in her heart no harm has come to you. All mothers do who care for their children."

"If I telephone her she'll know anyway," argued Roderick.

"What *is* telephone?" asked Janine.

"You mean you don't have one?"

"The word is not in our language."

"How do you send messages then?"

"What messages?" asked Keera.

"To your husband," said Roderick, "when he's away at work and you need to tell him something, or to people you know who don't live in the same area – friends and relatives in other parts of the country."

"If we needed him, Kern would know," said Janine. "And if the event was important the whole of Llandor would know, too. News travels, Roderick, even beyond the boundaries of our land. Were he interested, the Grimthane himself could have learnt of your arrival by now."

"But how?" asked Roderick.

Keera smiled.

"Minds have power," she explained. "We think and our thoughts are not our own, they touch whoever is around us. And the air we breathe is full of images, not just from us. The trees whisper and the birds make songs of all they know...and the animals convey, for good or ill, whatever affects them. When the oak coiled its roots round the girl and you put fire to it, we knew. We knew from the squeak of the mouse, the cry of the leaves, the shriek of the grasses – although not many hear and understand, as we do, the natural voices of the land."

"As you do, Mother," Janine corrected.

"As I do," Keera replied.

"So you *do* know what I'm thinking!" said Roderick.

"Only the essence of your unhappiness," said Keera.

"I'm not unhappy now," said Roderick.

Keera laughed. "If you were," she said, "I would know I had failed in my purpose. Who dwells under my roof, in the halls of Woodholm, soon forgets his sorrow." She fetched an earthenware tureen from the shelf, filled it with stew and set it on the table.

"They come," she announced. "But none too willingly, I deem. The experience of their own world and fears of this one cloud their judgement somewhat. Or else they do not know how to trust."

A moment later the door opened.

And Kern ushered Craig and Carrie inside.

"You've no right to bring us here!" Craig said angrily.

"We want to go home!" said Carrie.

"Later," said Kern.

"Now!" said Craig. "And where on earth are we anyway?"

"Woodholm," said Roderick.

And they spun to face him.

"Fatso?" said Craig.

"Is it really you?" said Carrie.

"We thought you were dead!" said Craig.

"Sorry to disappoint you," Roderick said coolly.

"We thought you were behind us," Carrie explained. "We didn't know you weren't there until the wolves caught up with us. How did you get here?"

"With me and Festy," Janine said curtly.

Carrie stared at the girl and her mother.

"This is Janine," Roderick said proudly. "And this is Keera. They're friends of mine. We're safe here and they've invited us to stay the night."

"*I'd* rather go home!" Craig said fiercely.

Keera smiled gently.

"Of course you would," she said soothingly. "And later we will discuss it. We'll do whatever we can to help you. But now you are chilled and hungry. Come, sit at our table and eat before the stew grows cold."

They sat on the wooden benches, Craig, Carrie and Roderick opposite Janine and her father, as Keera ladled the stew into dishes. Roderick could hardly wait to begin. Spoon in hand, he was poised and ready. But suddenly Keera paused in her serving, as if she were listening.

"Who guards the door?" she asked.

"Festy," said Kern.

"And where are the others?"

"They patrol the woods to the north."

Janine regarded her worriedly. "Mother? What is it you feel?"

Keera shook her head. "Just shadows, perhaps, beyond the boundaries of this land. A movement – a gathering...I know not what. Mayhap it has nought to do with us."

"And mayhap it does," Kern said darkly.

Keera made no reply.

She placed the dish before Roderick, gestured to Craig and Carrie. "Eat," she commanded. "Don't wait for me or mine."

The stew was meatless, Roderick discovered, but delicious anyway, the most wonderful food he had ever tasted, stock thickened with vegetables, hot and spicy, and fragrant with herbs. He finished the bowlful before the others had hardly begun, wiped it clean with chunks of bread and, at a nod from Keera, helped himself to more.

"Pig!" said Craig. "You need a trough, not a plate!"

"No wonder you're so flaming fat!" said Carrie.

"Is that why you hate Roderick?" asked Janine.

"Because he eats to console himself and is overweight?"

Carrie glanced at her and bit her lip.

"We *don't* hate him," she said uncomfortably.

"We just tell the truth," said Craig.

"There are kinder ways of telling the truth," Janine retorted. "Such thoughtless remarks can be very hurtful."

"I don't care what they say anyway!" muttered Roderick.

"Are you sure you do not care?" asked Keera. "Is that not the root of your unhappiness? You heed what others say and hate yourself because of it. And all that is good in you is buried even from your own sight. Small wonder you are sad, Roderick. If you want to be liked you must first begin to like yourself, I think."

Roderick stared at his plate. For some reason he had lost his appetite. And did he really hate himself as Keera said? The room had gone uncomfortably silent, Craig and Carrie chastised and himself, too, in a way. No sound but the kettle singing softly, the chink of cutlery and the warm whispering of fire. Then, clearly in the distance, Roderick heard the howling of wolves.

Kern rose to his feet.

"Something is out there!"

"No," said Keera. "There is nothing, Kern. They merely sense, as I do, the stirring of a thing."

"You mean the Grimthane?" said Janine.

"What's the Grimthane?" asked Craig.

"The Fell One," said Roderick.

"What do you know about it?"

"Janine mentioned him before."

"So who is he then?"

Carrie shuddered. "I don't think I want to know," she muttered.

"You are wise," said Kern. "Who and what the Grimthane is need not concern you. Tell me instead how came you into Llandor?"

They stared at each other.

Somehow Roderick sensed it would be best not to tell everything, although he wanted to. It would be easy to blame Craig and Carrie for what had happened, say they had threatened him when he had trodden on Carrie's biro by mistake. But that kind of petty bickering had no place in Woodholm. If Roderick told tales to Kern and Keera it was he who would become detestable, not Craig and Carrie.

"It was an accident," said Roderick, and he saw the relief in Carrie's eyes.

"We didn't mean to come here," she said.

"We were fooling about," said Craig.

"Then Roderick fell down a slope," said Carrie. "And we followed – just to make sure he was all right."

"We must have come through some kind of

gateway," said Craig.

Kern sighed.

"I feared as much. Unstable things, gateways, now here and now gone. Never, to my knowledge, has a door between worlds opened into these woods before."

"You mean we can't return home by the same route?" asked Craig.

"It remains to be seen," replied Kern. "For those who gain access to these lands there is seldom a quick release. Gwillym the Mapper remains here still for all his years of searching."

"You mean we're stuck here?" asked Carrie.

"For the rest of our lives?" said Craig.

"It mightn't be so bad," said Roderick.

Craig rounded on him.

"I've got my first driving lesson next week!"

"And I was going to a disco on Saturday!" said Carrie.

"And what about our exams?" said Craig. "We've only got one more term! This could ruin my whole future!"

"And that's not all!" said Carrie. "People are going to think we're dead! My mum will have called the police by now! She'll be going through hell!"

"There's no telephone," said Roderick. "I've already asked."

Tears trickled down Carrie's face.

"We can't stay here!" she sobbed. "I don't like it here. That tree...those wolves...the Grimthane... everything scares me! Please! You've got to help us!"

Keera rose from her seat. She knelt beside Carrie, cradling her in her arms.

"Forget the Grimthane, child. You are safe enough here in Woodholm. And the wolves will not harm you. As for the tree – there are few of its like in Llandor. But come with me. I will show you your room and the bathing pool, brew you a tea with herbs that will sweeten your sleep. In the light of a new day things may seem different. Tomorrow we will search for the gateway that will take you home. Who knows? It may be waiting for you still."

Roderick watched as she led Carrie away. Somehow he knew they would not find the gateway however long they searched. Their lives were in Llandor now and nothing would ever be the same again.

CHAPTER THREE

Carrie awoke in the dim blue light, huddled naked beneath the quilt, and for a few moments wondered where she was. The room was small and windowless and bare as a prison cell. It contained no furniture, just a mattress on a stone shelf on which she lay, and a niche in the wall that held a hairbrush and comb and an arrangement of flowers and leaves in an earthenware vase. Her clothes, and the rough hessian towel she had used last night, hung on hooks behind the door, and her school bag stood in the corner, all indistinct shapes in the semi-darkness.

The previous night Keera had given her a sleeping draught to help her forget, but now she remembered. Roderick Burden had trodden on her biro and she had ganged up with Craig against him, followed him through the woods. Then she had fallen into the clutches of an oak tree that tried to pull her down into the earth, been chased by wolves and ended up here at Woodholm. There must have been a doorway, Craig had said. And everything familiar was gone – her home, her friends, her family in Ditchford, the comprehensive school in Lydminster and all she had planned to do with her life. She was trapped, maybe for ever, in a strange world that contained God-only-knew what horrors.

She cried, softly, but her tears were useless. The grief remained, and so did her fear. She wanted her mother, wanted Keera to come and comfort her, wanted to sleep again and forget. But she was awake now, and her thoughts plagued her, and the confines of the room grew more and more claustrophobic. She had to get out, she decided, had to do something to occupy her mind and pass the time until morning. Finally, remembering the bathing pool, Carrie draped the towel round herself and opened the door.

The light was dim and blue in the hall too, a semblance of night where the flowers slept and the carpet of grass was cool beneath her feet. But the air remained warm, almost humid, as she approached the pool. Fronds of ferns growing by the doorway brushed against her legs, and the leaves of a rowan tree that arched above it dripped with moisture as she passed beneath. Blue steamy heat rose from the surface of the pool. And someone was there before her – a fat white body wallowing in the water.

Roderick stinking Burden. Carrie stared at him with revulsion. She could see the pale rolls of flab round his midriff and his sagging chest with breasts that were bigger than her own. Hardly surprising he had refused to bathe with the rest of them, she thought. And she remembered sitting next to him at the dinner table, the sour smell of his sweat and his sly farts that had put her off her food. She could not understand why Keera and Janine had chosen to defend him, taken his side against Craig and herself. They could not possibly like him, thought Carrie. No one, if they were honest, could like Roderick Burden. He was a horrible boy, a creep, a coward, a sneak – thick and stupid and useless at everything – the last person Carrie would have chosen to be stranded with, either in her own world or another. She turned in disgust and headed back to her room.

She dressed in her school clothes – a grey skirt soiled by yesterday's experience, a scarlet prefect's sweater and navy blue blazer – and picked up her bag. She would wait in the kitchen, she decided, and do her Physics homework prior to leaving. But as she brushed her hair, studied her dim reflection in the mirror, there was a quiet knock at the door. She ignored it, in case it was Roderick, but it opened anyway and Craig entered the room. He, too, was dressed in school uniform and clutching his bag of books, as if this was the beginning of an ordinary day and they were both about to walk to the end of the lane and catch the bus to Lydminster.

"You're awake then?" said Craig.

"I couldn't sleep any more," said Carrie.

He glanced at his digital watch.

"It's half-past six anyway. If we leave now, it ought to be getting light outside. We can head back up through the woods and look for the holly thicket."

Carrie pondered. She felt safe here, but the woods scared her. She would never forget that tree and her own terror. There were marks on her legs, raw red weals where the roots had gripped her, soothed by Keera's ointment but not yet healed. And it was not just the trees that worried her.

"What about the wolves?" she asked.

"They're tame, aren't they?" said Craig.

"And what about Roderick?"

"I'm not hanging around waiting for *him*," said Craig.

"But we can't just leave him here! That's mean!"

"You'd rather team up with him than come with me?"

"Don't be stupid!" said Carrie.

"Then you'd better make your mind up," said Craig. "Because I'm getting out of this place right now, even if I have to go without you."

He turned and opened the door. And Carrie had no time to think. She saw Roderick's bare buttocks disappearing into an opposite room and went with Craig, their footsteps silent on the grass, silent on the bare earth floor of the passage. Slowly, quietly, Craig drew back the bolts and opened the door, closing it quietly behind them.

The outside air was freezing. Hoar frost whitened the landscape, and dawn streaked the sky with fiery colours. The river chuckled coldly over its stones. And the wolf arose like a shadow from its bed of rushes, shook the rime from its pelt, and moved to bar their path. Feral eyes stared at them. Its breath made smoke, and saliva dripped from its tongue.

Craig stepped boldly towards it.

"Good boy! Nice Festy!"

The wolf's hackles rose.

"It's not going to let us pass," said Carrie.

"In that case we'll go in the other direction," said Craig.

They turned their backs on Festy and the morning sky, followed their own shadows westwards along the river bank and took the first narrow path they came to that led upwards into the trees.

Everything glittered in the gathering light, leaves and branches and bracken iced with white. Carrie's feet froze, her face ached with cold, and uncomfortable feelings churned in the pit of her stomach.

They were wrong to leave Woodholm, she thought, and even more wrong to leave Roderick behind. He could not help being fat and unlikable and, despite what Craig believed, it was not his fault they had ended up in Llandor. What had happened on the bus had been an accident but she and Craig had pursued him, seeking revenge. And now they were abandoning him, sneaking away without a word, an act of treachery that made her feel rotten inside. If something nasty happened it would serve them right, she thought.

But the woods seemed tranquil enough, the trees faceless and sleeping, everywhere gripped by an eerie stillness. No sound but the rush of the river behind them, their steps among the leaves and a rustle of wings in the high branches. She looked up. A solitary crow flapped and swayed and finally settled. Its raucous cry was loud in the silence and was echoed by another some distance ahead. Their presence unnerved her.

"Let's go back," she begged.

"Why?" asked Craig.

"Because I don't like it," said Carrie.

"You're just being neurotic," Craig told her.

The path levelled and divided.

"Have you any idea of the way?" asked Carrie.

"It's along here," Craig said confidently.

"Are you sure about that?"

"I'm not absolutely one hundred per cent certain," Craig admitted. "But it looks familiar, and I'm sure I recognize those rocks." He pointed. "Look, there's the slope beyond them with the holly thicket at the top."

"You mean we're nearly home?"

Carrie felt a surge of joy and relief as she followed Craig along the narrow path between the outcrops of rock. Tumbled boulders were green with lichen, taller than she was, with cracks and crevices showing dark beneath them and tree roots clinging to them like claws. They gave way, at last, to the leaf-filled hollow, and she could see the slope down which Roderick had fallen, skid marks in earth and the gloom of the holly thicket above.

Craig gave a whoop of triumph and headed towards it, with Carrie behind him, slipping on leaves where the frost turned to dampness and clutching her bag of school books. Then there were claws indeed, talons hooked in her hair, and she screamed as the crow attacked her. Craig turned back, swung his bag as the black wings flapped. The contents scattered and the bird shifted its attention from Carrie to him. He beat it away, beat it as Carrie went on screaming, and the woods filled with sudden sound as if the trees themselves hissed and gibbered. Then on lazy wings the crow retreated, sailed away to the safety of the tree-tops, leaving them stunned and shaken.

"Why did it do that?" wept Carrie. "Crows don't attack people, not deliberately."

"That one did," said Craig.

He picked up his books and pens and pencils.

"Are you hurt?" he asked.

"No," she sobbed.

"Then let's get out of here."

He gripped her hand.

It was not far to go, just a quick scramble to the top of the slope. But there were movements in the holly thicket – hands parting the branches – and, suddenly, staring down at them, was a row of mean little faces. And when they looked round, the hollow was ringed by similar faces, peering at them from among the rocks and behind the trees. The colour drained from Carrie's face and she stared in horror.

The creatures were vaguely human in shape, small and skinny with grey warty skin, pointed ears and round milk-white eyes. Their heads were bald, and their grinning mouths showed rows of vicious-looking teeth. They were dressed alike in short leather tunics, and each one carried a two-pronged spear. Hissing and gibbering, urging each other on, they advanced menacingly towards Craig and Carrie.

"Goblins!" said Craig.

"What do they want?" moaned Carrie.

"Us?" said Craig.

"I knew we should have stayed at Woodholm!"

"We're going to have to fight them, Carrie!"

"What with?"

"Use your feet. Knee them in the crotch or kick their teeth in!"

Her voice rose hysterically. "There's too many of them! We don't stand a chance!"

Craig's grip on her hand tightened, and the crow cackled in the tree-tops. The goblin creatures grinned and advanced, their spears held at the ready. Then, from somewhere in the woods above them, where Ditchford ought to be, Carrie heard the howling of wolves. Her voice quavered, then gathered strength.

"Festy! Lodi! Jag! Here, boys! Here, Benna!"

They came through the holly thicket as if in answer, poured down the slope in a quick grey tide, a whole pack of them, howling and slavering. She did not know if Festy led them or not. She saw death in their bared fangs and savage eyes, and thought it was her own. But the wolves ignored both her and Craig. Ferocious and snarling, they launched themselves at the goblins.

Carrie did not wait to witness the battle. All she saw were a few moments of terror – spurts of bright blood on a grey pelt, a torn throat. The air was filled with shrieks and cries, the yelping of wolves, howls of pursuit as the goblins turned and fled. Craig tugged at her hand. Then she, too, was running, following him back along the path between the rocks and brambles, and away into the open woods.

They ran without stopping, without pausing to glance behind. And the path led downwards as it had before, down and down through frosted trees to emerge, finally, in the sunlight of the valley where they paused for breath. The river chuckled over its stones and the woods were quiet above them, devoid of menace. Still trees glittered and the sunlight slanted between them, pale and golden, as if nothing bad had happened there and never could. For a moment Carrie wondered if she had dreamt it, but there was a scratch on Craig's hand where the crow had attacked him, and memories of goblins in her mind that would not fade for all the brightness of the morning.

Left and right she gazed along the river bank, and it seemed they were nowhere near Woodholm. In the north she saw a range of mountains rising beyond the hills, snow-capped peaks as high as the Austrian Alps. She gazed at them in growing dismay, for the first time recognizing the difference between this world and her own, the impossibility of escape. Goblins guarded the gateway through the holly thicket and everywhere was Llandor, as far as she could see.

"Which way do we go?" Craig asked her.

"Does it matter?" she said dismally.

"We've got to find our way back to Woodholm, Carrie."

"You intend to join up with Roderick again?"

Craig shrugged. "We've got no choice, have we? Obviously we're all in it together, whether we like it or not."

"You should have thought of that before!" said Carrie.

Craig glanced at his watch. "It's still only half-past seven," he said. "With a bit of luck no one will even know we've been gone."

"*We'll* know," Carrie said curtly.

Abruptly, she turned away from him and marched along the river bank towards the mountains. From now on, she thought, she was going to make her own decisions, not go blindly wherever Craig led. Then she was aware of her own loneliness and the fear of being by herself. She glanced behind, saw Craig following, and her fear fled. Together, yet not together, they kept to Carrie's chosen path. Beside them the bright water danced and runnelled over its stones, and small birds fed on the seeds of willow herb, and frost on the trees melted in the sun. For a while Llandor seemed almost pleasant. But there was no sign of Woodholm and soon Carrie began to worry. They were going in the wrong direction, she thought. And, as she rounded a bend, she saw houses with shingled roofs, a water mill and a few open fields. There was someone walking along the river path towards her. She stopped nervously in her tracks and waited for Craig to catch up.

"Who's that?" she asked.

"It's not Kern," said Craig.

The man was younger than Kern, taller and leaner with long straggling hair and a beard, nondescript brown in colour. He wore a sweatband round his forehead, a white shirt and a brown hessian cape, and hessian trousers tucked into knee-length boots. He carried a luminous orange backpack on a tubular frame, as if he were a camper looking for a camp site, come there by mistake just as Craig and Carrie had done.

"He's from our world!" Carrie said excitedly.

"I wouldn't bank on it," said Craig.

"You can't buy a backpack like that in Llandor."

"How do you know?" asked Craig.

"Because it's nylon, isn't it? And there aren't any factories here. No telephones or modern facilities, remember?"

The young man waved to them.

He seemed friendly, eager to meet them.

Then, from the woods, the wolves came leaping to surround him and Carrie moaned, thinking they would tear him to pieces, closed her eyes against the horror. But Craig squeezed her arm in reassurance, and she saw the man was still alive, the wolves pawing his clothes, their tails wagging in welcome. He laughed, petted them in turn, thrust them aside and strode on along the path as they frisked round him.

"Well, Festy! Well, Benna! Fine guardians you are, indeed to goodness. You will be licking me to death before I have even breakfasted! Shift your carcass, Jag, and let me pass! Out of the way, Lodi bach."

"He's Welsh!" said Craig in delight.

And when he reached them he confirmed it, dropped his backpack on the ground and shook their hands. His name was Gwillym Jones, he said. He had been studying cartography at Bangor University until he got lost in the mist in the wilds of Snowdonia on a rambling holiday. He had camped for the night on Cader Idris and woken to find himself in Llandor.

"It was August 1960," he said.

"You mean you've been stuck here for almost thirty-five years?" said Craig.

"Five years," said Gwillym.

"But it's 1994 now," said Carrie.

"October 14th," said Craig, glancing at his watch.

Gwillym stared at them.

"Thirty-five years! Thirty-five years have gone in only five summers? I know time moves differently here but I never suspected..."

His fists clenched at his sides and his face twisted as if he was in the grip of some overwhelming emotion. The wolves whined sadly, seeming to share what he felt, and Carrie felt a lump of pity rise in her throat. His voice, when next he spoke, was soft and appalled.

"They could be dead," he said brokenly. "Mam and Da – they could be dead – and my little brother grown to be a man and Glenys wed to someone else, her children older than I am. And I must be dead to them, too, thirty-five years dead and forgotten."

"I'm sorry," whispered Carrie.

Craig stared at his watch. "It should only be the 13th," he said.

Bewildered, Gwillym shook his head. "I was not thinking of something like that. I was thinking this was a holiday, see? I was just taking advantage of it – travelling round from place to place, making maps and waiting for the gateway to open that would take me home. I never dreamed thirty-five years could go by. I never imagined..."

"Are you Gwillym the Mapper?" asked Craig.

"Heard of me, have you?"

"Kern mentioned you last night."

"You are staying at Woodholm then?"

"Just temporarily," said Craig.

"When did you arrive?"

"Yesterday," said Carrie.

Gwillym smiled a little bleakly.

"It may not be too late then? Even after thirty-five years it may not be too late to go home. The Seers were predicting that a gateway between worlds would open in the foothills of the northern mountains and I came here quick as I could. Return together, we can, back to our own Earth."

"That might be easier said than done," Craig said glumly.

"What do you mean?" asked Gwillym.

"The gateway could be closed already."

Gwillym's face clouded.

"Are you sure?"

Carrie shuddered. "We've just been back there."

"And only the wolves came through it," said Craig.

"And goblins," whispered Carrie.

"Goblins?" said Gwillym.

"They were going to attack us," Carrie said tearfully.

"Until the wolves attacked them instead," said Craig.

Gwillym stared at them. Then he gazed about him at the morning sky and the surrounding hills, the village behind him and the autumn trees in all their flaming colours – reds and russets, browns and golds. No sound in the land but the singing river and a young girl calling from the village, no movement but the runnelling of water and the millwheel turning. Even the wolves lay still, their eyes fixed on Gwillym's face, patient and adoring, dried blood staining their pelts.

"Is it true?" Gwillym murmured. "Are there goblins here in Llandor? I had thought they were not to be found on this side of the northern mountains. Something's afoot then. And if the Grimthane is behind it we had best not be lingering here in the open."

"Who *is* the Grimthane?" asked Craig.

Gwillym shouldered his pack.

"No one I would wish to meet," he said. "Nor you either, boyo, if you have any sense. We had best be taking ourselves off to Woodholm and reporting to Keera. She will be knowing what's about and what we should do. And maybe the gateway's open still, so let's not be giving up hope, shall we?"

Whistling to the wolves he strode away, and Craig and Carrie had no choice but to follow. Hurrying to keep pace, they retraced their steps back along the river bank the way they had come.

High in the sky above their heads a single crow sailed like a scrap of burnt paper. And Carrie's fear grew greater than all her losses.

CHAPTER FOUR

The hall was empty when they arrived. Until Janine came racing across it.

"Gwillym! You've come back!"

She hurled herself into his arms and, just for a moment, Carrie envied her. She was at home in her own world and glad to see someone, as Carrie felt she could never be as long as she remained in Llandor. She was imprisoned there and all her friends were elsewhere, except for Craig and Roderick, who were imprisoned with her and Roderick had never been a friend. He stared at her from the kitchen doorway, fat-faced with sly piggy eyes and a peeved expression.

"Where've you been?" he demanded.

"Out," said Carrie.

"For a walk," said Craig.

"Gwillym, meet Roderick," Janine said joyfully.

"So there are three of you?" said Gwillym.

"And we're waiting to start breakfast," said Roderick.

Food was all he cared about, thought Carrie, but she did not say it. The fact that she and Craig had tried to return home without him still troubled her. It was an act of meanness worse than anything Roderick might have committed, and it was bound to come out before long. She went to her room, dumped her school bag in the corner and sat on the edge of the sleeping shelf, chewing her fingernails and not wanting to face people.

Even through closed doors she heard the anger begin – Roderick's voice, shrill and accusing, Craig arguing defensively, Janine scathing, Gwillym condemning. After a while Kern shouted for quiet and banged his fist on the table. There was a moment of silence, but then they began again, their raised voices louder and angrier than before. It was a kind of madness, thought Carrie, and all that had happened was her and Craig's fault. They had brought a hatred into Woodholm where none had existed before, infected Janine and rekindled in Gwillym something he might have forgotten. Her fists clenched and she wanted to scream at them to stop it.

Then she heard the opening of the kitchen door, an instant hush and Keera's indistinguishable words, soothing, calming, setting things right. And the quietness spread, unravelling the tight knots of Carrie's nerves and stilling her emotions. The sense of her own wrongness remained inside her, but now she had the strength to handle it, the courage to make her own peace. Slowly her fists unclenched. She knew what she had to do and there was no excusing herself. Strangely determined, she rose from her bed and crossed the hall to the kitchen.

They were seated at the table, bowls full of steaming porridge before them. They all looked at her, but no one spoke, although Keera smiled a greeting. Warmth from the fire coloured Carrie's cheeks but it was no shame to apologize where an apology was due, no shame to admit she had been wrong. She faced Roderick squarely, noticing the surprise on his face, the puzzlement in his eyes. Actually he had nice eyes, she thought, patient and accepting and hazel in colour, as if another Roderick dwelt within him, not fat and petulant, but a decent, likeable person. And maybe it was not she who had betrayed him but he who betrayed himself. Nevertheless, she owed him something, and her voice stayed steady as she spoke.

"I'm sorry, Roderick. We shouldn't have tried to go home without you. It was a rotten thing to do. Please forgive us."

There was no more to be said.

The silence intensified, and Roderick gaped at her as she sat on the wooden bench beside him, picked up her spoon and helped herself to honey.

"It's a lovely morning," said Carrie. But the silence went on, grew more and more uncomfortable, and no one else was eating.

"Is something wrong?" she asked.

"You could say that," Janine retorted.

"Let the cat out of the bag good and proper, you have," Gwillym told her.

"How do you mean?"

Roderick slammed down his spoon.

"Craig said you tried to wake me! He said you knocked at my bedroom door but I never answered! And that's why you went without me! The flaming liar!"

Carrie glanced at Craig. "I didn't know..."

"Big mouth!" snapped Craig.

"And there we have the truth of it," Janine said coldly.

"Pretty nasty behaviour, indeed it is," agreed Gwillym.

"I hate them!" Roderick said furiously.

"Let's not start again," begged Kern.

"I said I was sorry," mumbled Carrie.

"What good's that?" howled Roderick.

"It's better than no apology at all," said Craig.

"Hush," said Keera. "Wounds are best healed by silence, not words. Finish your breakfasts, all of you."

They continued their meal, but Carrie stared at the dish of porridge and felt sick to her stomach. She had tried to put things right and made the situation worse, exposing Craig for a liar, stirring up the hate. Roderick was right. It was no good being sorry. Words could not change what she was or what she had done. The wrongness remained, a part of her nature, an evil she had brought from her world into this.

"How can you want to go back there, Gwillym?" Janine finally asked. "How can you want to return to a world where people behave like this? Where they hate each other and betray each other? Where there is no liking, no loyalty, no truth or trust?"

Gwillym sighed. "I suppose I belong there, see?"

"It's where we all belong," said Craig.

"Until you love as I do," Kern said quietly.

Gwillym stared at him. "You mean you-?"

Kern nodded. "I too came from your world," he said. "I was a woodsman there, in a time so long ago I have almost forgotten. I was made to fight in battle for the cause of a king whose name I hardly knew. Among a hundred men from the same manor, we marched to join with other hundreds from other manors, soldiers all of us who were not bred to be. I cannot recall the field on which I fought, but in the slaughter I received a wound from which I might have died, had I not woken in Llandor in my lady's arms."

"She healed you?" asked Gwillym.

"She did," said Kern. "But that was far away in Irriyan. And when I was well and strong again we travelled here to Woodholm. Since then I have been a free man, Gwillym. I am not bound in Keera's service as once I was bound to serve the man who called himself my master. I am here of my own will and affection. And never could I desire to return to serfdom in the world from which I came."

"It's not like that now," Gwillym assured him.

"Not in England anyway," said Craig.

"The young rebel," said Gwillym. "They march in their thousands, denouncing war and singing songs of peace."

"Not any more they don't," said Roderick.

"The nineteen sixties are nostalgia now," said Craig.

"And our modern music is rubbish," said Roderick.

"No, it's not!" said Craig.

"It is according to my mother," said Roderick.

"All young people are selfish according to my mother," said Carrie. "And there are wars everywhere, and rapes and muggings and bombings and murders..."

Anguish flickered in Gwillym's eyes. "Things have got worse then?"

Janine sniffed. "No wonder the Grimthane stirs and whets his lips!" she said.

"Enough of that, daughter!" Kern said firmly.

"They cannot stay here with us, Father!"

"Nor will they. Not for long."

"So what's going to happen to us?" Roderick asked in alarm.

"Nothing," said Keera. "Nothing for now. You must trust us, Roderick. We will do all we can to shield and harbour you. Meanwhile, Kern will search for the gateway through which you came. Mayhap you can return to your own world unscathed by this experience."

Kern rose from the table. "Let us hope that possibility remains," he said.

"May I come with you?" asked Gwillym.

"I'll show you where it is," Craig said hurriedly. "And if it's still open we'll come back and fetch you," he said to Roderick.

They made ready, Gwillym putting on a royal-blue cagoule from his pack, and Kern donning his long, shimmering cloak and grasping his woodsman's axe for protection. They left within minutes, but Carrie knew what they would find. The gateway was closed and they would be stuck in Llandor for the rest of their lives, as unsettled as Gwillym – remembering the world they had lost – unless they loved, as Kern loved Keera, and forgot. But she could not imagine that. Years and decades stretched before her, devoid of purpose. And how could she possibly sit there forever and do nothing? She spooned up the sweet luke-warm porridge, then raised her head.

Keera was gathering the dirty dishes.

"Shall I do the washing up for you?" Carrie offered.

"There is no need," said Keera.

"But we've got to do something," Carrie said desperately.

Understanding dawned in Keera's eyes. Waiting in idleness was never easy, and even household chores had a therapeutic value. Carrie could help Janine, she said, and Roderick too. There were the chickens to feed, the goats to milk, cheese to churn, water to be fetched from the well, the garden to tend, and vegetables to dig and pick and prepare for the evening meal. In Woodholm there were always things to do and it might raise their spirits to be out in the open air.

For a moment Janine looked hostile. Then she

shrugged. "We'll feed the chickens first," she said.

"I'm allergic to feathers," Roderick announced.

"Then you can fill the water buckets and help us in the garden," said Janine.

"Work off some of your flab," Carrie said cuttingly.

Outside the back door was a yard with a well, barns and a dovecote, hewn from the hillside along with the house itself. Morning sunlight slanted through the trees that grew on its roof, and beyond the garden and orchards were meadows full of wild flowers and pale swaying oats. Scents filled the air of all the intermingled seasons – bluebells, apple blossom and lavender. And over it all a yellow light shone, warm as summer, from a sky that was maybe no sky at all.

"It's magic," breathed Carrie.

"It's Woodholm," Janine said, matter-of-factly.

"It's still magic," said Carrie. "And if I can't ever go home, I wouldn't mind living in a place like this. It makes Llandor seem bearable."

Janine glanced at her and Carrie saw sympathy in her eyes.

"Living here is hard work," she said warningly.

Roderick was obviously allergic to work as well as feathers. Chickens were better frozen and wrapped in cellophane, he muttered, and the smell of goats' milk made him feel sick. He did carry the pails to the dairy, and he did offer to shut the field gate after Janine and Carrie had driven the goats to pasture, and he wound the windlass to haul the water from the well. But he sprained his wrist lifting the bucket from its hook, vanished into the house with an expression of agony on his face, and was not seen again for several hours.

After they finished the chores in the dairy, Carrie and Janine attacked the garden, hoeing and raking and weeding, working together in companionable silence. Carrie dug carrots and potatoes, placed them in a trug, and Janine spread compost and pulled up the pea haulms. It was pleasant at first. Bees buzzed round the marrow flowers. Small birds fluted in the orchard and white-winged butterflies danced above the cabbage patch. But the day grew warmer and the work harder. Carrie removed her red school jumper, undid the buttons of her blouse and rolled up her sleeves. And strands of fair hair that had escaped from Janine's plait were darkened by sweat. Soil smudged her face, and the shimmering tunic she wore was stained with strawberry juice, the almost colourless material reflecting green and scarlet among the bean rows in a perfect camouflage.

"It's not nylon, is it?" Carrie asked her.

"It's elven cloth," said Janine. "My mother weaves it."

"Elven?" said Carrie. "You mean there are elves in Llandor?"

"Keera for one," said Janine.

"Then you're—?"

"I'm half elven," said Janine.

Carrie stared at her for a moment, as if she were only half human as well, then looked away in embarrassment.

"Do you make and grow everything you need?" she asked.

"Don't you?" asked Janine.

"We buy most things from the supermarket," said Carrie.

"Here we are many days' walk from the nearest market," Janine informed her. "But most years, in the spring, a group of peddlers pass this way trading their wares and bringing us news from other parts of Llandor."

"And where do you go to school?" asked Carrie.

"I learn from my parents," said Janine.

"It's all very different from our world," said Carrie.

"I think I would not like your world," said Janine.

"And I don't think I'll ever get to like this one," said Carrie.

"Maybe you won't have to," said Janine.

She was trying to be kind, thought Carrie, trying to be reassuring, but both of them knew she would never get home to Ditchford. In a different world, to a different way of life, she and Craig and Roderick would have to adjust. And already there were blisters forming on her hands. She straightened her back, thought of the bathing pool and Keera's ointment, and stared across the garden. And did she imagine a chill in the air? Gathering clouds beyond the canopy of light and the grey woods encroaching on the far edges of the meadows?

Janine followed her gaze, and her eyes looked troubled. "There's going to be a storm," she said.

"Is that bad?" asked Carrie.

"Not if that is all it is."

"What else could it be?"

"Probably nothing," said Janine, but Carrie thought she lied.

Roderick came from the house.

"Keera says you're to lock up the chickens, shut the goats in the barn and come inside."

Janine nodded grimly and hurried to obey.

Carrie dumped the laden trug at Roderick's feet. "You can take that inside," she told him.

She hauled open the barn doors as Janine whistled in the chickens, then followed her to the field to fetch the goats. The sky had grown darker and the distant woods loomed nearer, as if Keera's magic were slowly withdrawing, letting in the outside world and whatever it contained. A chill wind ruffled her hair as she returned with Janine to the house.

Roderick was still standing in the doorway, gazing at the sky with narrowed eyes. "What's happening?" he asked.

"There's going to be a storm," Janine repeated.

"What kind of storm though?" Carrie asked worriedly.

Janine bolted the back door at top and bottom. "Whatever it is, Woodholm will protect us," she replied.

"It's something to do with the Grimthane, isn't it?" Carrie persisted. "He's after us, isn't he? Because of what we are?"

"What do you mean?" Roderick asked nervously.

"I think it's something we've brought with us," Carrie said unhappily. "Something inside us from our world that isn't right here. A kind of evil."

"I'm not evil!" Roderick said indignantly.

"It's not just you," said Carrie. "It's all of us, Roderick. Me and Craig as well. We're... not very nice people, are we?"

"Speak for yourself!" said Roderick bitterly.

Without even bothering to pick up the trug of

vegetables, he turned away and headed for the kitchen, his heavy tread crushing the grass and flowers of Keera's hall, his words crushing Carrie's hope. He couldn't see, did not want to see, they were all as bad as each other.

"We're going to have to leave, aren't we?" she said.

"Sooner or later," Janine confirmed. And her blue elven eyes looked unexpectedly sad.

CHAPTER FIVE

"Would you really have left Roderick behind?" asked Gwillym.

"No," lied Craig. "Of course we wouldn't."

"Carrie seemed to think..."

"Carrie doesn't know me."

Gwillym smiled. They climbed and re-climbed the slope to the holly thicket, ducked through dark branches looking for the gateway, until both of them were bound to accept it was no longer there. Gwillym never said what he felt. Each was alone with his own separate thoughts in a silence of mutual respect. Then, reluctantly, they went to join Kern, who was searching the hollow below. Nothing remained of the goblins except a few torn fragments – a tattered tunic, an abandoned spear and a couple of crow feathers lying among the leaves. Black sheen in the sunlight caused Craig to remember. Before the goblins came Carrie had screamed and the crow had attacked them.

"Quite deliberately," he said.

Kern's face darkened. "Crows and goblins? Working together in a concerted effort? I have never heard the like of that before."

"Are you thinking what I'm thinking?" asked Gwillym.

"It speaks for itself," said Kern.

Gwillym nodded. "The Grimthane is behind it, right enough."

Craig stared nervously round the hollow.

"What would the Grimthane want with me and Carrie?"

"Perhaps we should attempt to find out," said Kern. "And if we learn what the Dark Lord intends for you, mayhap he will lose his advantage."

"How are you going to do that?" asked Gwillym.

Kern whistled to the wolves, set them to search around the rim of the hollow. They had been trained to protect humankind, he said, and were not indiscriminate killers. Once the goblins took flight they would not have followed. It was likely that the majority had escaped, headed back to the bolt holes from where they came. And, as goblins were no lovers of daylight, wherever they were hiding could not be too far away.

"You mean we're going goblin hunting?" asked Gwillym.

"We need to know what they know," said Kern.

"They'll kill us!" said Craig.

Kern laughed, and ran a finger along the sharp blade of his axe. "Goblins are cowards," he said. "Ruled by fear, as are most of the Fell One's minions. They will run from my axe, not face it. And had they wanted to kill you, they would have done so already. I suspect they had orders to take you alive..."

"But you can't be certain of that!"

"And the order will not be applying to me anyway!" said Gwillym.

"We're not looking to capture the whole horde," said Kern.

Gwillym shook his head.

"Craig and I are not even armed, see?"

"Well, that's easily remedied," said Kern.

He surveyed the saplings that grew beneath the larger trees, chose two for their straightness, felled them, trimmed them, and presented them to Craig and Gwillym. Armed with a stout staff and stripped of their excuses, they surveyed each other. Where they came from they had never been called upon to fight, not even in their own defence.

"I'm a pacifist," protested Gwillym.

"So am I, from now on," said Craig.

"When it is kill or be killed," said Kern, "you will do what you must. Now let us go and find ourselves a goblin." Up among the tumbled rocks a wolf howled the direction, and Craig glanced at his watch. It was ten to eleven when they set out through the trackless woods following the scent. Barred sunlight shone through the trees, melting away the last traces of frost, and the air was almost warm, although Craig had no time to enjoy it. Kern was a woodsman born and bred, and Gwillym had been trekking through Llandor for the past five years. But Craig's only physical exercise was once a week on the school football field and he had a struggle to keep up.

The woods grew wilder, the way steeper, the underlying land more rugged, pitted with old stone quarries and abandoned mine workings. It was iron-ore country, Gwillym said. And now and then he paused to make notes in a vellum pocket book with the stub of a pencil, allowing Craig a brief respite before Kern urged them on, clambering over rock falls or forcing a path through tangled undergrowth, following wherever the wolves led.

Craig was breathless and sweating, scratched by brambles, stung by nettles, for the first time knowing how Roderick felt – fit for nothing and shaking from the effort. Evenings and weekends spent sitting on his butt reading fantasy books or playing games of heroes and quests on his computer had ill-prepared him for the reality. After an hour of hiking through Llandor, he felt ready to collapse.

Then the wolves lost the scent, howling round the perimeter of a flooded quarry. Walls of sheer stone, where ferns clung to the cracks and crevasses, cradled the black, brooding water below. There was no way down without crampons and a rope. Kern surveyed it as if he intended to try, until a wolf cry in the woods beyond urged him once again to follow. The cloak he wore shimmered in shades of brown and grey and yellow, reflecting the landscape round him in a chameleon camouflage, and Craig almost lost sight of him as he topped the rise and strode relentlessly on across the next wooded ridge.

"I thought he said it wouldn't be far!" he protested.

"Straight up, it isn't," said Gwillym.

"I bet we've walked five miles already!"

"Less than two by my reckoning," said Gwillym. "And maybe three thousand feet up from the river. No more than a league as the crow flies, see?"

"Well, I'm not a crow!" said Craig.

"Get used to it, you will."

"I don't bloody well want to!"

"That's how I felt once," said Gwillym.

It was enough, perhaps, that Gwillym understood. It gave them something in common – both of them snatched from the same world, their lives wrecked because of it. But Gwillym had had time to adjust, he was less emotional and had found a purpose here – Gwillym the Mapper, doing what he would have done anyway. Craig's future seemed ended before it had begun.

"What's it like?" he asked.

"What?" asked Gwillym.

"Living in Llandor?"

"Everything's much simpler," said Gwillym.

"How about technology?"

"Wind and water mills," said Gwillym. "Nothing more."

And what use was a potential computer expert in a world without technology? thought Craig. From Lydminster comprehensive school he could have gone on to university, but here he had no hope, no earning potential, no chance. Vicious and hating, he slashed at the undergrowth with the wooden staff, and followed Gwillym up the slope.

As they climbed higher, the broad-leaved trees gave way to fir and the going grew easier. Now, with Kern still ahead of them, they climbed through an evergreen gloom and over a brown carpet of pine needles, where nothing grew except fungi – gelatinous growths on fallen branches, blobs of brown and frills of pallid white and speckles of lurid orange. Behind them the sunlight vanished and the air smelt sour and cold, of death rather than life. No birds sang in the silence, and nothing moved apart from themselves and the wolves who led them.

"I don't think I like it here," said Craig.

Kern turned his head. "We are leaving Keera's sphere of influence," he said.

"Is it wise to continue?" Gwillym asked, worriedly.

"Will you be turned from the Trineway for fear of a few goblins, Mapmaker?"

Gwillym's teeth flashed white as he smiled, and his eyes shone.

"The Trineway?" he breathed. "You mean we are near it?"

"Aye," said Kern. "If my senses are true, it lies ahead. But whether we can reach it from here remains to be seen."

"What's the Trineway?" asked Craig.

It was Gwillym who answered him, told him of the three lands, Irriyan, Mordican and Llandor, and the ancient road that had once united them, the Trineway, on which Gwillym had not yet set foot. Across bridges, over chasms, up flighted stairs and mountain passes, through tunnels beneath them – the Trineway led from the plateau of Irriyan in the west, branched north into the barren wastes of Mordican and eastwards on to Harrowing Moor in Llandor.

Who built it were the giants of legend, lost long ago in time, and no one was certain how much of it remained passable since the Grimthane's coming. Woodholm and the Rillrush valley was as far north as anyone in their right mind would want to go, said Gwillym, except for a few stalwart dwarfs who refused to be ousted from their mountain strongholds.

"Dwarfs?" said Craig.

"Likely it was dwarfs who mined these woods," said Gwillym.

"What about elves?"

"Apart from Keera, it is unusual to find an elf outside the bounds of Irriyan," said Gwillym. "They are not great travellers, see?"

"You mean Keera's an elf?"

"It is elven magic that makes Woodholm what it is."

"And are there wizards and orcs and ringwraiths as well?"

"There are wraiths," said Gwillym. "But I have never seen one. They are dwelling mostly on Harrowing Moor or in the Marrans by the southern coast. And there's an Enchantress in Seers' Keep, and a resident sorcerer, and a few wandering mages. Trolls are in the Northern

Marches, and orcs in Scurry. Orcs are sea-trolls, sailors of the open oceans, and none finer once you are getting used to their appearance."

Craig stopped walking and leant on his staff. His leg muscles ached and his mind seemed unable to grasp the things he was hearing. The beings Gwillym spoke of were inhabitants of books and fairy-tales, not reality. And was Keera really an elven woman?

"Did you ever have trouble believing?" Craig asked Gwillym.

The Mapper shook his head.

"If something's real you are bound to believe it, otherwise you are beginning to doubt your own senses, your own experience. This world is as real as ours was, Craig. I've walked it, touched it, mapped its contours..."

"So how do you explain it then?"

Ahead of them Kern and the wolves effectively vanished in the evergreen gloom, and Gwillym shrugged, speculated as they went on walking.

"The Seers say it is a parallel universe, this world and ours occupying the same space. They say that in the past the boundaries overlapped and the inhabitants of this world spilt into ours and left their legends and, over the centuries, we have strayed here to form the human stock. They could be right, I suppose."

"Who are the Seers?" asked Craig.

"Stay long enough in Llandor and doubtless you will be meeting them. Strange powers, some of them have – the power of foreseeing future events, or foretelling a person's life. Others can scry across distances and some can predict when a gateway will open between our two worlds."

"You mean they'll be able to tell us how to get home?"

Gwillym sighed.

"If they predict soon enough and we can reach the gateway in time. All the way from Kellsdale I was trekking here. I left the moment their message came and still I am missing the moment. And once the Seers themselves could control the gateways at will but now, they claim, that power is lost to them."

"And you believe them?" asked Craig.

"Why should I not?" asked Gwillym.

"They could be lying."

"For what purpose?" asked Gwillym. "And would Keera lie? It is not in her nature, I think, and she is one of them. And had you stayed in Seers' Keep, as I did for a while, you would not doubt their integrity. They are dedicating their lives for the good of all who dwell in these lands. They, it is, who hold the Grimthane at bay. Without them...Yaaaah!"

Gwillym gave a gargled cry, and clutched Craig's arm as a net fell from the trees, enmeshing them both. Craig thrashed, trying to extricate himself, but the net tightened and swung, and he and Gwillym fell together in a tangle of arms and legs. Their staves snapped beneath their weight and they were hoisted high above the pine forest floor, dangling there helplessly, howling for Kern to rescue them. He came at a run but there was nothing he could do, nor the wolves either.

Suddenly the surrounding trees revealed their ambush. Ropes uncoiled and, with fierce cries of triumph, a host of squat little men came sliding down from the higher branches. There must have been twenty or more, miniature warriors bearded and helmeted, breast-plates gleaming, armed with axes and hatchets and short swords made of beaten metal. Menacingly, weapons raised in readiness, they closed in on Kern and the wolves, moved to attack – until he raised his hands in supplication.

Then they stopped.

"Dunderhead!" said one.

"Dolt!" said another.

"That's no goblin!" said the third.

"It's Kern the woodsman."

"Keera's man!"

"She who is lady of these woods!"

"Guardian of the Rillrush Valley."

"Stay your arms, brothers!"

Several of them bowed to Kern.

"Our apologies, squire."

"Sincere and unmitigated."

"A genuine mistake it was."

"Short-sighted above ground, we are."

"No ill was intended to those in Keera's favour."

Kern nodded.

"What of my companions?" he asked.

"We'll let down the net, squire, never you fear."

"Keep your wolves at bay and we'll let it down."

"Now! At once!"

Craig clung to the mesh, felt the net sway and give. A dozen pairs of hairy hands controlled the rope, lowered him gently to the ground. They were dwarfs, he supposed, no higher than his shoulder, swarming around him, removing the traces, until finally he stepped free. Deepset eyes under bushy eyebrows peered up at him and Gwillym from a dozen swarthy faces. Bulbous noses sniffed at the air. In gruff voices the dwarfs discussed them.

"No goblin reek, brothers."

"Human, they be, to our way of telling."

"But not of Llandor."

"Not of our world."

"Come from the other, they have."

"This one a while ago."

"And this one newly arrived."

"Smelling of strangeness, he is."

"Yet each bear the scent of Keera's halls."

"My lady gives them shelter," said Kern. "And he who knows the scent of Woodholm must be a friend indeed. We have not met before to my remembering, but allow me to introduce Craig from the other world and Gwillym the Mapper."

"Gwillym the Mapper?"

"Here's Gwillym the Mapper, brothers!"

The dwarfs whispered his name, and a stout red-bearded warrior stepped forward.

"My name is Diblin," he declared. "I'll be the spokesman, with your permission, brothers." The other dwarfs nodded. "We are honoured to make your acquaintance, Master Gwillym. Who works with the Seers and charts our lands has the respect of us dwarfs, right enough."

Gwillym bowed solemnly.

"I hadn't realized I was famous," he said.

"We expect you to chart our dwarven halls in time," said Diblin.

"And what brings you down from your mountain fastness?" asked Kern. "It is no sudden love for our woodlands, I'll be bound."

Diblin spat.

"Goblins, that's what! We saw them before dawn, an armed band of them heading down the Trineway. Followed them, we did, and set our trap for their return. Not goblins we netted, though, was it? So where are they? Where are the cowardly muckle-headed band of slime-suckers?"

"Have they not returned this way?"

"No sniff or sign of them," growled Diblin.

Kern shook his head.

"We must have been following their downward trail!" he declared.

"You mean they have escaped by another route?" asked Gwillym.

"What about that flooded quarry?" Craig suggested. "It's where the wolves lost their scent for a while. Maybe they took to the water?"

"Water," hissed Diblin. "Water to hide their stinking footsteps! Dolts and dunderheads, brothers! We should have thought of that! And mayhap they are skulking there still, waiting for cover of darkness to wend their way home. Can you lead us there, woodsman?"

"My wolves can," said Kern.

"Then let us join forces," said Diblin fiercely. "The Grimthane is stirring. The air bodes ill and I feel him in my bones. Things are afoot and us dwarfs need to find out what."

The other dwarfs nodded.

"That was our purpose, too," said Kern.

"Then let's not waste time," said Diblin.

Kern gestured to the wolves, sending them loping back down the slope on silent paws. The dwarfs coiled their ropes, folded their net and went scurrying after them. Craig and Kern made to follow, but Gwillym lingered, staring wistfully upwards into the deepening gloom of the pine forest. His breath smoked in the chill air.

"We are so near," he murmured.

"There are things more urgent than the Trineway," said Kern.

"Those dwarfs can handle the goblins without our help."

"I mean the weather," said Kern.

"It's turning cold," said Craig.

"Unnaturally so," said Kern. "The breath of the Fell One, Gwillym. He comes to protect his own, I fear, and hide their traces. We would be wise to head for Woodholm as quickly as possible. Unlike the dwarfs, we are not equipped to withstand what the Grimthane might unleash against us. The Trineway must wait for another occasion."

Gwillym turned away, accompanied them down the slope without further protest. Dwarfs and wolves had already vanished from view and a breath of wind whined eerily above the tree-tops. Craig shivered in his thin school blazer, and the gloom increased, dark and eerie, until they could barely see each other's faces.

When they emerged from the cover of the fir trees the snow was already falling, huge white flakes whirling through the more open forest. Wind lashed the trees and the undergrowth visibly whitened, changing the landscape until even Kern seemed unsure of the way.

The blizzard worsened. Head bent, Craig followed blindly in Kern and Gwillym's footsteps. The chill wind chaffed him. Snow froze to ice on his face and his body grew numb, his limbs leaden. Tree roots tripped him and every step he took required effort, became a fight against his own inertia and the strange sweet lassitude that gripped his mind.

He did not remember falling. He did not remember anything until the caress of a hand and a voice murmuring his name brought him briefly back to consciousness. He was lying on his pallet in the small cell room, blankets covering him and a hot stone at his feet to warm him. His toes and hands thawed and throbbed with pain. From beyond the partly open door he heard the gruff voices of dwarfs, a clatter of crocks in the kitchen, Janine and Carrie's chatter, and the yelp of a wolf. Then Keera held a cup to his lips – hot bitter brew that flowed through his blood like fire and caused him to cough.

"What happened?" he spluttered.

"You became lost in the storm," Keera told him. "The wolves found you buried in the snow and the dwarfs carried you home. But you are safe now, Craig. Safe in Woodholm with me."

She was elven, Gwillym had said, and a Seer as well. The lady of the Rillrush valley, the dwarfs had called her. She would not lie...and her blue eyes assured Craig of that. He was safe enough with her – safe for ever as long as he stayed in Woodholm. Her hand stroked his forehead.

"Sleep," she murmured.

And he closed his eyes.

CHAPTER SIX

Later Craig awoke. The light was dim blue and the stone at his feet still retained a vestige of warmth. But through the half-open door a draught of cold air gusted on to his face. Briefly, he heard the wild rush of the river and the whine of the wind that suddenly ceased, voices whispering in the hall and a stamp of feet, as if someone had just come in from the night. He listened, but could not make out what was said. The only clear sounds were the rumbles of hunger in his stomach informing him he had missed his supper.

Two-thirty by his watch. He pulled on his underpants, draped a blanket round his shoulders and headed for the kitchen. The grass in the hall was cool beneath his feet. Blue steam issued from the bathing pool and a shaft of yellow candlelight came from a nearby room. Voices murmured within – Kern and Keera and Diblin the dwarf, holding a late-night conference. Curious, his hunger momentarily forgotten, Craig approached.

It was a large room with whitewashed walls, empty of furniture except for a stool and a weaving loom where Keera sat, with a length of shining material draped across her lap. Snow dripped from Diblin's beard and dropped from Kern's shoulders, melting in a dark pool at their feet. Before them, Gwillym squatted on his haunches, his head bent in concentration, scratching at the earthen floor with a sharpened stick. The others watched him intently.

"We're here," said Gwillym. "Here's the Rillrush valley and here's Woodholm. And here's Seers' Keep – almost due south."

"How far?" asked Keera.

"Well over a thousand miles," said Gwillym. "That's four hundred leagues to you. Our most direct route would be to head for Dornaby, take a river boat down the Kellswynd to Kellshaven, then take passage on a clipper and sail round the coast to Seers' Keep. Unless we go east to Scupper's Key and set sail from there."

"That way you will have to cross Sedge Marsh," warned Keera.

"I can handle a few boggarts," growled Diblin.

"You won't be needing to," said Gwillym. "There are navigable channels across Sedge Marsh, see? And plenty of barges plying the waterways between Droon and Scupper's Key. I went that way before, the last time I visited Woodholm, and it's possibly quicker. Less walking distance to Droon than to Dornaby and for their sakes we are bound to consider it. They are new to Llandor, unused to the privations of a non-technological society, unseasoned travellers who will not take kindly to untold miles of forced marching."

"Tenderfeet!" muttered Diblin.

"They will march if needs must," said Kern.

"Indeed they will," murmured Keéra.

"But you would still feel easier if we head for Irriyan?" Gwillym asked her.

"It is the nearest haven," Keéra replied. "The elven land where no evil can enter. They will be safe there for as long as needs be, and Kellsdale is a kinder land through which to travel."

"It's the detour north that I don't like," growled Diblin. "The snow lies deep beyond the mill bridge and the woods are accessible from Mordican too. They could harbour the Fell-One alone knows what. At your request, lady, I have agreed to journey with them and protect them if the need arises, but one dwarf is no match for an army! And southwards to the ford the Rillrush valley is clear, us dwarfs have checked it – Kern too, with his wolves."

"So why not keep our options open until we have crossed the ford?" Gwillym suggested. "East, south or west, all are possible and if the ways be clear we can make our decision then."

Keera sighed. "I bow to your decision, Gwillym. You have travelled much and know the different routes better by far than I do, and 'tis you who will be leading them."

"Whatever way we go," growled Diblin, "we need to be setting out as soon as maybe, before the Fell One makes another move against us."

Craig drew back. The blue light shadowed him and his fists were clenched, a huge resentment growing inside him. With Carrie and Roderick, he was being shipped out to some unknown place at the earliest opportunity, and he had no say in the matter.

Simmering with annoyance, he went to the kitchen. It was warm and empty, full of yellow light, and preparations were under way in there as well. The table was laden with earthenware jars containing dried fruit and nuts, pickled eggs and gherkins, a round hard cheese and a stack of flat bread still warm from baking. A wooden airer stood by the fire-pit draped with woollen socks and hessian shirts and trousers, thick woollen jackets and long hooded cloaks fashioned from the same shimmering material Keera wove on her loom. There were hessian backpacks, too, piled on the floor, and several pairs of goatskin boots. A griddle smoked, and the remains of the stew simmered in the pot.

Craig took a dish from the shelf and helped himself, cleared a space at the table and sat down to eat. Around him the silence brooded, as if the whole of Woodholm slept. Yet he could feel a tension in the air, a loss of stability, a sense of imminence.

Leaving, he thought, all three of them, their wishes and desires of no account.

The experience was familiar to Craig. It stripped him of the status he had gained at Lydminster comprehensive and reduced him to a child again, having to do what he was told regardless of what he wanted. And Llandor should have been different from that, a fantasy land of good against evil, where Craig would have some vital part to play in overcoming the Grimthane. Instead, he was being sent from harm's way to wherever Gwillym and Keera decided, and denied the opportunity.

He considered his own counter-argument. If there was a war going on he ought to be allowed to take part. Not physically, perhaps – he did not want to kill anyone personally, not even a goblin, but strategically he might be useful. All the books he had read, all the hours he had spent mustering his forces on the computer, had to be good for something. Whoever was running things and doing the organizing might be glad of Craig's help. He could offer his services to the Lords of Llandor, to the King or the Prince, or whoever it was who ruled the land. One day he might even become important, rich and famous and rewarded with a title and his own estate, a Lord himself. The thought cheered him, gave him a reason for being there, a sense of purpose.

Then, out in the hall, he heard Janine's voice.

"I want to go with them," she said.

"Why would you wish that?" Keera asked curiously.

"Because I want to be with Gwillym," said Janine.

Keera laughed. "Gwillym is a wanderer, and always will be," she said.

"And your place is here!" Kern said sternly. "You have much left to learn before you leave us, daughter."

Their voices faded.

Janine was being treated as a child too, thought Craig. She was expected to do as she was told, the same as he was. And a moment later she entered the kitchen and dumped a basket of apples on the bench beside him. Her expression was sullen and her hair was a mess. Fair straggles escaped from her plait, and the front of her tunic was white with flour as if she had been up all night cooking and baking, with no time for sleep and no time to tend to herself. She made no attempt to speak, just set about parcelling the food into separate packages.

"What's going on?" Craig asked her.

"Nothing as yet," she retorted.

"If it concerns me," he said, "I've a right to know."

Janine shrugged.

"You'll be leaving," she told him.

"When?" he asked.

"Whenever Keera decides."

"Without being consulted?"

"I'm not being consulted either!" Janine said curtly.

It was Craig's turn to shrug.

"Our leaving is not going to make any difference to you," he said. "You'll be staying here, won't you?"

Janine made no reply, but her lips tightened as she cut the cheese into wedges.

Craig watched her. "Do you always do as you are told?" he asked.

Again she did not reply. And again he watched her – pickled eggs and gherkins being distributed between the separate parcels of food, her blue eyes thoughtful and brooding.

"Why?" he asked finally.

"Why what?"

"Why are we being bundled off in the middle of the flaming night without so much as a by-your-leave? What's so blasted urgent it can't even wait until morning?"

"Maybe it *will* wait until morning," Janine replied.

"Now answer my question, please."

Janine sighed.

"Woodholm isn't a fortress, Craig."

"What's that got to do with it?"

"Keera can't protect you, not for long."

"Against the Grimthane, you mean?"

"He has only to raise an army..."

"Then in that case she needs all the help she can get."

Janine shook her head.

"You don't understand," she said. "Once you are gone, the threat will be averted and Woodholm will be safe."

Craig stared at her.

Her slim hands mixed a bowlful of nuts and raisins.

And he could not believe what she said.

"What are you getting at, Janine?"

"Is it not obvious? It's you he wants, all of you or one."

"And he'll raise an army if we stay?"

"If he deems it necessary," said Janine. "There is no telling what the Grimthane might do to enforce his will. His ways are not predictable."

"But we can't be *that* important, surely."

"It depends on your purpose here."

"We don't have any purpose. We came here by accident. We told you that."

Janine shook her head.

"Gateways don't open by accident, Craig. Llandor admits who Llandor needs and everyone comes here for a purpose, although they may not know it."

"So there isn't a war going on then?"

"Just you and Carrie and Roderick," said Janine.

And the Grimthane wanted them – all of them or one – and everything that had happened was entirely personal. Uncounted questions flittered through Craig's head, and fear trickled through the nerves of his stomach and dried his throat.

"So who is he?" he demanded. "Who exactly *is* the Grimthane?"

"I've been told not to discuss him," said Janine.

"Why?" asked Craig. "If it's us he's after, we need to know what we're up against, don't we?"

Janine said nothing for a while, just fetched the backpacks and stowed away the parcels of food, added several apples to each, then left the kitchen with the empty basket. Opting out of answering, Craig supposed, but she returned a few moments later carrying a large earthenware flagon which she placed on the table. She glanced at him thoughtfully, took a jug from the shelf and unstoppered the flagon, releasing a sweet, winey smell. He watched as she filled the jug. Rich golden liquid streamed through the light and was poured, slowly and carefully, into half a dozen goatskin bottles. And finally she spoke.

"No one knows who the Grimthane is," she said. "And no one knows what. Whoever enters the realm of Mordican does not return. Mayhap he is human and mayhap he is not. A shade, perhaps? Or a formless entity? I only know what I have heard, and what the rumours tell. He is the Evil One who cannot die, a hunter of souls who searches for his own reflection. In winter storm and summer drought, in wind and fire and flood and pestilence, he moves among us. All things that live are prey to him. And all men serve him who serve their own base natures and uncontrolled desires. Does that answer your question?"

Craig shuddered.

"You mean he's the Devil?"

"He is there in your world too?"

"Not like that," said Craig.

Or maybe he was, he thought. Maybe he was there in the murders people committed and the terrorist killings, all the wars in the world and the famines in Africa – the Devil, like the Grimthane, working his will through anyone who would serve him. But he was not real in the way he was in Llandor, a power to be reckoned with and fought against. He was a concept Craig had never really considered, not a protagonist like the Grimthane, the Fell One, hunter of souls, hell-bent on hunting him and Carrie and Roderick for his own evil ends.

He shuddered again.

"You need not worry," Janine assured him. "He will not succeed. I doubt if anyone in Llandor or Irriyan would assist the Grimthane's purpose. Be they elves, dwarfs or humans, they will all help you escape from his clutches."

"Escape where?" asked Craig. "Who's going to take us in after what you've told me? If Keera can't protect us then who else can? We could be running for the rest of our lives!"

Janine frowned, stoppered the goatskin bottles, and added them to the contents of the backpacks. Then she spread sleeping bags on the floor, rolled them and tied them. And she might have been speaking to herself anyway.

"Inside ourselves we are all running and hiding from the Grimthane," she murmured. "Each and every one of us, throughout our lives. We are none of us invulnerable – not the Seers in their Keep, not Merganna the Enchantress, no elf or dwarf, nor Kern or Keera or me. We all of us must run, or hide, or fight in our various ways. You and

Carrie and Roderick are not alone, and by helping you we maybe help ourselves somewhat, at least that's what we hope. Why else would Diblin leave his mountain home and Gwillym agree to lead you? Why else would I want to leave Woodholm..."

Her words trailed away. She glanced at Craig as if she hoped he had not heard or understood, then thrust the bedrolls in the backpacks, secured the straps and stacked them ready for departure. There were six, Craig counted. One each for himself, Carrie and Roderick, one for Gwillym and one for Diblin. And Kern, he presumed, would be travelling with them. Suddenly it all seemed so final, and their stay at Woodholm had been so brief, little more than twenty-four hours – or so he thought, until he pressed the date button on his wrist watch.

October 20th. In Earth time they had been in Llandor almost a week. He tried to imagine it: the police searching the woods looking for his body, his father making a television appeal for news of his whereabouts, his mother hysterical with grief or under sedation, and his younger brother poking around in his bedroom, fiddling with his computer. It couldn't be true, he thought. It couldn't be happening. Yet it was. And he did not want to know any more, did not want to think, or care, or feel. He rose from his seat, tore the watch from his wrist and hurled it in the fire-pit. And when he turned to look at Janine he was crying.

"I'm going back to bed!" he said.

She nodded dumbly.

For the pity in her eyes he almost hated her, her and Keera and everyone else he had met. But most of all he hated Llandor, the world he had come to that offered him no future and no place. He returned to his room, but he had hardly settled on the sleeping shelf, hardly got his feelings back in order, when the dim blue light brightened through green into yellow and Gwillym entered. He placed a bundle of clothes, warm from the airer, on the foot of Craig's bed.

"Want to talk about it?" he asked kindly.

"No," said Craig.

"Janine is telling me..."

"Janine doesn't bloody know!"

"Your parents, is it?"

"It's everything!" Craig said savagely. "I don't want to be here, Gwillym!"

"Nor did I," said Gwillym. "But as we are here it is better to accept it and make the best of things than begin to hate it. And you will like it at Seers' Keep..."

"That's where we're going, is it?"

Gwillym nodded.

"Be leaving shortly, we will. Whenever you're ready, see?"

"Do Carrie and Roderick know?"

"Keera is telling them now, I think. We will be leaving our own things here in Woodholm and there is breakfast in the kitchen if you are wanting it."

"I've only just had supper," Craig said sullenly.

Gwillym clapped him on the back.

"So keep your pecker up, boyo, and don't be long."

He left the room and for a few minutes Craig rebelled. He did not want to go to Seers' Keep – and why should the Seers want to harbour him? The whole plan was stupid – stupid setting out in a snowstorm in the middle of the night on a thousand-mile journey without knowing for sure if they would be taken in. It was better to stay here and fight it out, but that would hardly be fair on Keera and Janine. It was their home that stood to be destroyed if the Grimthane came. And how could anyone withstand an army of goblins and the essence of evil? This was not a computer game, it was real, and however Craig looked at it, from whatever point of view, he was sure he could not stay.

Reluctantly, he left his bed and dressed in the unfamiliar clothes, lashed the trousers tightly round his legs with leather thongs, pulled on the goatskin boots and donned the thick woollen jacket. Everything that made him what he was –

the clothes he normally wore, his blazer and school bag and all that linked him to his former life – would be left behind. Now, he looked like a serf, and the transformation was a kind of grief. His whole identity seemed gone. A stranger, even to himself, he returned to the kitchen.

The other two were already there. Carrie was yawning over a dish of porridge, with Roderick beside her, stuffing his face. He looked fatter than ever in the woollen jacket. Thick, thought Craig, in every sense of the word, void of comprehension and whining to Gwillym across the table. It was dark outside, he complained, not yet morning and snowing like billy-o. And there were goblins about.

"The goblins have gone," Gwillym assured him. "Kern and the dwarfs have checked downstream as far as the ford and there's no sign of them. And Diblin will be coming with us anyway. No self-respecting goblin is likely to tangle with him. And the snowstorm will cover our footsteps, see? With a bit of luck we'll get clear away without the Grimthane knowing."

"You mean he'll think we're still here?" said Roderick.

"With a bit of luck," repeated Gwillym.

"Then why can't we stay here anyway?"

"You know why," said Carrie. "Keera explained. She isn't able to protect us. If we stay here and the Grimthane comes, and she refuses to hand us over, Woodholm could be razed to the ground. You don't want that to happen, do you, Roderick? So we've got to go, haven't we?"

Impressed by Carrie's understanding and impressed too by her quiet acceptance, Craig sat listening beside her. She glanced at him briefly, and her eyes were as grey and calm as Gwillym's and totally fearless. Suddenly he admired Carrie. She had guts, he thought, which was more than could be said for Roderick Burden.

"A thousand-mile walk will do you good, Fatso."

Roderick stopped eating. His face was pale and pimply, and alarm showed in his eyes. His voice was a squeak.

"A thousand miles? I can't walk a thousand miles!"

Craig smiled at his discomfiture. "You're going to have to," he said cruelly.

"We can take our time," said Gwillym.

"Why can't we take a bus or train?" asked Roderick.

"Because there aren't any," said Gwillym.

"So we'll be walking," Craig said with relish, "a thousand miles through rain and wind and snow, through boggart-infested countryside, carrying two tons of supplies on our backs. And by the time we get to Seers' Keep you'll be that thin you won't even recognize yourself. Skin and bone, Burden, providing nothing nasty gets you on the way and you survive at all."

Sweat beaded Roderick's upper lip, and Craig could smell his fear.

"Did you have to tell him that?" Carrie asked crossly.

"It's true," said Craig.

"No, it's not," said Gwillym. "It's not true at all, see? There's nothing nasty living in Llandor that I've come across. And once we reach Dornaby we can take a boat down-river as far as Kelshaven. After that, it's only about three hundred miles to Seers' Keep."

"And will we be safe there?" Roderick asked anxiously.

"You will be safe," Keera said from the doorway. "Once away from here you will all be safe. Diblin and Festy will guard you, and wherever you travel no harm will come to you. And now, if you are ready..."

Carrie smiled trustingly, and Roderick was stupid enough to believe anything, but Craig was not so easily fooled. He shouldered his backpack, donned one of the shimmering cloaks and pulled up the hood, following Gwillym into the hall where Kern and Diblin were waiting, knowing Keera had lied. He noticed the short-sword strapped to Diblin's back, a knife at his belt and coils of rope round his waist. He noticed the freshly honed edge of Kern's axe. He noticed the wolves, their feral eyes and their air of expectancy. And Keera said they would be safe? That no harm would come to them? She was lying, lying through her teeth, thought Craig. Then, suddenly, she was standing before him for the ritual leave-taking. Her hands clasped his hands and her blue eyes stared into his own.

"Goodbye," she said. But her thoughts said more than that, soft words whispering in his mind.

"If I have lied, Craig, I have lied for a reason and you will say nothing to the others of any danger. With my reassurances I have given them the only gift I can, the peace of Woodholm which they may carry with them in their hearts. Allow them to keep it for as long as they can, and say nothing of what you suspect. I ask you this as your gift to me. Promise me your silence, Craig."

Understanding her now, he nodded his agreement.

And she kissed his cheek.

"Good luck," she said softly.

Then she turned to embrace the others: Carrie, Roderick and Gwillym, each in their turn, speaking to them softly, smiling her encouragement, bidding them goodbye.

"Where's Janine?" Gwillym asked her. "Why isn't she here to say goodbye to me?"

Keera shook her head.

"Some partings hurt too much," she explained. "She hides herself away and hides her sorrow, but when I find her I will bid her farewell on your behalf."

"On behalf of us all, please," said Carrie.

"Tell her I'll be back," said Gwillym.

But Craig somehow knew that Keera would not find Janine in Woodholm. He had been with her in the kitchen, had watched her prepare the backpacks. Six of them, he had counted, and now there were only five. Kern, intending to accompany them only as far as the ford, was not wearing one. Once again, this time unknowingly, Keera had lied. And once again, Craig kept silent, suspecting he might be to blame His own words, and a vision of Janine's blue eyes, seemed to haunt him as he walked into the night. Do you always do as you are told? he had asked her.

CHAPTER SEVEN

Grey dawn showed in the sky, and the blizzard had ceased, just a few flurries of fine snow whirling through the air, showers from the trees caught by the wind or sudden avalanches from the snow-laden branches overhead. On the ground it must have been twenty centimetres deep, much more where it had drifted, its chill whiteness burdening the whole landscape, dragging at Roderick's footsteps as he followed doggedly after the rest of the group. He had realized the moment they set out that he could not possibly keep up. The best he could do was plod at his own pace, on and on throughout the night, the river flowing darkly beside him giving him direction, the snow wiping out the traces of the ones who had gone before.

His aloneness grew with the light. Now he could see what before he had only suspected: the river bank was empty in either direction and the only footprints were his own. Snow-covered hills rose on either side, cragged and remote, and the wild woods offered no hope of human habitation. Somewhere, he supposed, the others would stop and wait for him. Or maybe they would not, in which case he would be truly on his own. It did not bother him particularly. Inside himself he had been alone for the whole of his life. At some point he would stop walking, he decided, then turn round and head back to Woodholm.

Meanwhile, he continued, on and on into the morning. Now and then the long cloak tangled round his legs, forcing him to pause and unravel it, but mostly it flowed grandly round him, Keera's gift reflecting the whiteness of the snow, shimmering like the river and rendering him almost invisible, except for his trail unwinding slowly down the Rillrush valley to be seen only from the sky. And the sky was as empty as the land, its unbroken greyness sweeping from horizon to horizon, vast and silent.

Then, on lazy wings, a solitary crow appeared, drifting downwards like a smut of soot to land among the high branches of a nearby tree. Dark wings flapped as the branch bent and swayed, dislodging its snow in a rush of cold. Roderick looked up, and the bird's harsh cry startled him, echoed across the distances, but it was only a crow. After a while he grew used to it, its bead-bright eyes watching him, its black wings fluttering from tree-top to tree-top as if it followed. It was almost companionable, he thought, a dark scrap of life, something that breathed and moved and existed apart from himself.

Caark! Caark!

"I can hear you," Roderick told it.

Caark!

"Do you want something to eat?"

Caark! Caark!

"Time for a mid-morning snack," Roderick announced.

Deep and green, the river ran beneath a shelf of natural rock and the path was blown clean of snow. Here was a good place to stop, he thought, and struggled to free himself from the straps of the backpack. He set it on the ground before him, but before he could unpack or search for provisions, he heard someone calling his name, a human voice, faint and far away, mingling with the noise of the water. A figure, cloaked and hooded as he was, and indistinctly seen, appeared round the bend.

"Roderick!" yelled Craig.

"What?" shouted Roderick.

"What the hell are you doing?"

"Nothing!" shouted Roderick.

"So shift your stumps! We've been waiting for ages!"

The crow flew away.

And a dark shape stirred in the river's depths.

Roderick was heedless of either. Beneath his cloak he struggled to put the backpack on again, shuffled reluctantly along the bank towards the place where Craig was standing. His legs ached from hours of walking through the snow, the chill air made a pain in his lungs, and fear crawled through his guts. Nearby, in the water, the dark shape shadowed him. Eyes in the depths, fathomless and malevolent, marked his movements. Had Roderick known of it, or noticed it, his fear would not have been of Craig. And as he expected, Craig greeted him scornfully when he approached.

"Is this the best you can do, Fatso?"

"Sorry," huffed Roderick.

"You're slower than an arthritic snail!"

"I'm going as quick as I can!"

"The others are getting frostbite waiting for you!"

"They're not bound to wait for me, are they?"

"No," said Craig. "But knowing you, you wouldn't recognize a ford if you saw one."

"I would," said Roderick. "My uncle drives a Ford Mondeo."

"That's what I mean," said Craig.

Roderick glanced at him.

And Craig thought *he* was stupid?

"How far is it?" Roderick asked.

"How far is what?" asked Craig.

"The ford," said Roderick. "Where we cross the river."

Craig's lips tightened, devoid of humour.

"Another mile, perhaps."

"So don't let me keep you," said Roderick.

Something snapped.

"Listen, Fatso..."

"No," said Roderick. "You listen to me. I don't know what we're doing here, or why. But as we are here, and stuck with each other, we had better learn to get along. I don't like you any more than you like me, and I don't need your company. So let's stay away from each other. And you stop needling me. Right?"

Without waiting for an answer, Roderick waddled on along the river bank. He had never faced anyone like that before, never spoken in such a way. He felt weak and trembly, but the fear had lessened, evaporated through the pores of his skin in a reek of sweat. He felt almost cleansed, almost grateful, as if he had confronted himself, not Craig, and discovered a kind of courage. He realized then that he did not actually dislike Craig at all. He was not a prefect at Lydminster comprehensive any more, he was just a person with his own problems and his own prejudices which Roderick could do nothing about.

He resisted the temptation to look behind and make sure Craig was following, resisted the impulse to talk to him or try to gain his friendship. As alone as he always was, he trudged on down the Rillrush valley through the snow that was fast turning to slush. The air grew warmer. The wind that had blown from the north changed direction, came soft in his face as if the Grimthane retreated and gave up his hold on the land. Trees dripped, and the daylight brightened, and the grey clouds parted, letting through gleams of watery sun. Apart from the fact that he was hungry, Llandor was not so bad after all, thought Roderick.

He rounded the next bend. The hills dipped and the path grew soggy, and here there was almost no snow. Trees retained their damp autumn colours, the bracken beneath them sodden sepia, and the river in the distance sparkling over its shallows. The ford, Roderick supposed, where Kern and the wolves were waiting. Smoke from a cook-fire on the far side drifted towards him with a smell of grilled fish, and he started to hurry.

Craig drew alongside.

"You're right," he said.

"About what?" panted Roderick.

"We'll call a truce, shall we? Just for the duration."

"Ignore each other, you mean?"

"Or pull together," said Craig.

"How?" asked Roderick. "If I can't keep up, how are we going to pull together?"

"That's your problem," said Craig. He strode ahead, then called over his shoulder. "Just don't say I haven't offered, that's all!"

By a series of flat stones, Craig had already crossed the river when Roderick eventually arrived. The wolves wagged their tails, and Kern clapped him on the back, and loud cheers greeted him from the far bank. Over the water Festy whined and paced, restless to be off, and Carrie brandished a fish cooked on a stick as if it were bait. Roderick gazed longingly. He had only to step, leap from stone to stone with the water chuckling between them, leap and balance and leap again. But the stones were green and slippery with slime and he was not built for leaping.

"Off you go," Kern called encouragingly.

"I can't," said Roderick.

"You can if you try."

"The stones are too far apart."

"Your legs are far longer than Diblin's, Roderick."

"But I'll lose my balance," Roderick protested. "I've never been any good at this kind of thing. Isn't there another way across? A bridge or something?"

"Only the Mill bridge, leagues to the north," said Kern.

"What's the hold-up?" Gwillym shouted.

"Come on, Roderick!" shouted Carrie.

"There's nothing to it!" shouted Craig.

Roderick did not hear what Diblin muttered. He heard only the cold chuckle of the river, its swirling water waiting to receive him. But it was not much more than knee-deep – he could see the gravel shining at the bottom – the worst he would get was a wetting, he decided. Yet the river scared him. Its rushing water contained a power he did not understand and darkness lurked in the blue-green depths nearby.

"I can't," he repeated.

"Take off your cloak and backpack," Kern suggested.

He did so, reluctantly.

And Craig came racing across the stones to join him.

"Come on, Fatso."

"I'm just about to," muttered Roderick.

"You take yourself across. I'll bring your things."

The darkness rose.

On the opposite bank Festy whined frantically. And without stopping to think, Roderick leapt and leapt again, leapt and paused and swayed and leapt, Craig behind him, urging him on. They were almost halfway across when something broke the surface...something dark and monstrous, with nostrils like blow-holes and water streaming from its flanks. It was a kind of horse, a creature such as Roderick had never seen before, nor even dreamt of in the worst of nightmares. Weed tangled its mane, and its eyes blazed balefully, red as fire, and its lips curled, showing fanged incisors. Its hideous whinnying drowned Kern's warning cry, and Carrie's scream, and the wild howling of the wolves.

For a moment Roderick stood petrified. And the beast approached, rising from the depths to the shallows, its hooves scraping the gravel. Then, from both sides of the river, the wolves came snarling through the water – Festy, Lodi, Jag and Benna – in a four-pronged attack with Diblin roaring behind them brandishing his sword. The horse creature paused and lowered its head.

And Craig shouted, "Get out of there, Roderick! Quickly! Quickly!"

Roderick turned, arms flailing the air to keep his balance, leapt as Craig leapt, back towards the bank where Kern was standing. Vaguely, behind him, he heard the wounded yelp of a wolf, saw the bright blood swirl between the stones before he landed on his knees among mud and rushes. He had no time to recover. Unceremoniously, Kern hauled him to his feet.

"Run!" said Kern. "Head for the cliffs further on and wait for me there. Diblin! Get out of the water! Get out of the water, Festy! Jag and Lodi, come here to me!"

Roderick was running by then, running as he had never run before, away from the river, up among the rocks and trees to higher ground, with Craig behind him. Kern's shouts receded into the distance and still Roderick ran – ran until his breath gave out, until his legs failed and his heart pounded and blackness boomed in his head. Then he stopped. Gasping and heaving, he sank to the ground, sat with his head on his knees and closed his eyes. Everything hurt, every breath, every muscle, every heartbeat, every sickening sensation in his body. Sweat poured out of him. And he tried not to think of what had happened.

Craig draped the cloak round his shoulders.

"Are you all right?" he asked.

"I will be in a minute," wheezed Roderick.

"Whatever that thing was, it killed Benna."

"But it was after us," muttered Roderick.

"It could have been coincidence," said Craig.

Roderick shivered as his sweat grew chill.

Those red burning eyes had gazed right at him.

And it was not coincidence.

He raised his head.

"Did Diblin and Festy get away?" he asked.

"I can't see from here," said Craig.

"Kern said we were to wait at some cliffs."

"We'd better get going then...if you're feeling able."

Shakily, Roderick lumbered to his feet.

"You realize we're on the wrong side of the river?" he said.

"We'll just have to find another way across," said Craig.

Craig carried his backpack and they walked together through the sodden woods. They had little to say to each other even then, but a shared instinct led them on up the hill along a slanting path back towards the river's edge. It flowed through a canyon with cliffs on either side, but the ground was crumbling and dangerous and they could not get close. They headed inland again, saw Kern striding through the trees before them with Jag and Lodi at his heels, and followed where he led, across miles of rough countryside where the land steamed in the afternoon sun and the river made rainbows in the air and roared down its rapids.

Roderick had neither breath nor thought to spare for conversation. His whole being was engaged in the battle with his own body, the sick waves of hunger that churned inside him and the almighty effort of keeping up. Then, as the tree shadows lengthened at the first onset of evening, Kern headed for a spur of sheer rock that overhung the river and finally stopped. A hundred metres below, the Rillrush foamed and churned, but Roderick saw nothing. He sank, exhausted, on to a nearby boulder.

Moments later, after talking to Kern, Craig returned to sit next to him, unfastened the backpack, pulled the stopper from a small leather flask and handed it to him. He had to shout to make himself heard above the noise of the water.

"Kern says it's mead and you're to take a swallow!"

Roderick swigged and coughed. Sweet and strong, the fermented liquid landed like fire in his empty stomach, coursed through his veins, warm and reviving. His head spun pleasantly, and he might have drunk the lot had Craig not taken it from him. And the food rations were pitifully small: just a single flat bread and a wedge of cheese which they shared between them, enough to survive on but not nearly enough to satisfy Roderick's hunger. But Craig had charge of the backpack and he dared not ask for more. He needed water, too, to slake his thirst after more than twelve hours of walking...but the only water was below them, in the depths of the gorge growing dark with approaching night. The rising chill made him shiver and there was no way down, no way across, yet on the high spur of rock Kern and the wolves continued to keep sentinel.

"What's he waiting for?" asked Roderick.

"Search me," said Craig.

The answer came almost immediately. There were shouts across the river and Gwillym and Diblin appeared. A moment later a rope attached to a large stone was hurled across the chasm. Kern hacked off two lengths with his axe, looped the remainder high around a nearby tree and waved his hand. The rope moved and tightened, slanted downhill at an angle to be secured to another convenient tree on the other side. Of the shorter lengths Kern fashioned two separate swings which he tied to the rope at the top.

"That looks fun," Craig said cheerfully.

Roderick gazed at it in horror. Surely, he thought, he would not be expected to cross the river on that contraption? Swing down a thin rope with a hundred-metre drop beneath him? At his weight? But that was exactly what Kern expected him to do. Grim and unsmiling, the woodsman beckoned, and he had to obey. With a feeling of dread he climbed up the intervening rocks, folded the shimmering cloak for a seat, clung to the swing with both hands and lowered himself gingerly into place. The supporting rope dipped and sagged alarmingly and only a few metres of rocky ground remained between himself and the launch into space.

"Good luck," said Kern.

"See you on the other side," said Craig.

"This rope's not strong enough!" wailed Roderick.

"It's elven rope," said Kern.

"So just get on with it," said Craig.

Fear dried Roderick's throat. His sweat turned icy. And the wolves whined their encouragement. On the high ground opposite, Carrie waved, but he could not do it – he could not take those few final steps. Wild panic gripped him. He began to whimper, refused to take his feet from the ground. He would rather go back to the ford and take his chances, risk being torn to pieces by the water horse. But before he could leave the swing, Kern acted, gripped the ropes and sent him hurtling forwards into empty space.

Roderick had never known such terror – a sickening lurch off the edge of the cliff, a giddying rush of speed through the semi-darkness, his scream and his stomach left somewhere behind. The rope dipped downwards towards the white churning water below and he clung for his life. He was travelling too fast. Gwillym and Diblin tried to hold him but he felled them both, smashed against hard ground on the other side of the river. Then he was lying among grass and bracken, his whole body bruised and pulped and jolted. Nothing was broken, Gwillym said, after a brief examination. But then Craig came hurtling across the river in Roderick's wake and landed almost on top of him.

"Whoops!" said Craig.

"You're standing on my arm!" screeched Roderick.

"You should have moved out of the way," said Craig.

"I can't," groaned Roderick.

"It's only bruising," Gwillym insisted.

"And bruising will heal," growled Diblin. "Unhitch those swings now, Gwillym, and let us be going on our way. 'Twill be dark soon and we must needs find a place to camp the night."

"What's wrong with here?" asked Craig.

"With the world and its mother knowing where we are?" asked Diblin. "You might sleep easy in your bedroll, boy, but I would not. That water beast did not appear by accident, you know. It has been marking our passage. Down there in the gorge it is, at this very moment, and it knows where we are. We need to put a league or so between the river and us before we sleep."

"I can't walk any further," moaned Roderick.

"Looks like you'll have to," said Craig.

Diblin hauled in the length of rope, and coiled it round his waist, as Craig and Gwillym retrieved their backpacks from the bracken and Carrie and Festy came scrambling down the slope.

"Is Roderick hurt?" Carrie said.

"Yes, I am," whined Roderick.

But it made no difference.

"Help me get him on his feet," said Gwillym.

Roderick was in agony all over, his forearm crushed by Craig's foot, and an injury to his shoulder. But they were ruthless, all of them. They even made him carry his own backpack. And across the river Kern turned homewards with a wave of his hand, a shape in the darkness heading back up the Rillrush valley, the two surviving wolves loping beside him. With him went Roderick's last link with Janine and Keera and the warm comfort of Woodholm. Except for Festy, the soft, sad crying in the wolf's throat, the shared pain of separation that was worse than any physical hurt.

Only the river sang with the beast it harboured, its shrill whinnying echoing from the cliffs, to be carried by the wind towards the north. Diblin was right, Roderick knew that. It was sensible to get as far from the river as possible before they pitched camp. He sighed his acceptance and limped wearily through the trees behind them.

Night fell swiftly over Llandor. From moonlight and starlight and the watchful eyes of the Grimthane's spies, the dark woods shielded them. But someone followed. Roderick heard footsteps in the leaves trailing behind him and turned his head. For a moment he could see nothing – until his eyes adjusted to the flicker of dark and light beneath and nearby trees where someone was standing. His voice was a screech.

"Who's that? Who's there?"

The person stepped forward.

"I'm coming with you," said Janine.

CHAPTER EIGHT

They camped among the trees that night, ate a sparing supper of bread and cheese washed down with water from a leather flask, and spread their bedrolls on the ground. After eighteen hours of walking they were all too exhausted for conversation, too weary to decide if Janine should accompany them on their journey or not. They simply accepted she was there, accepted that Keera would have found the note expressing her intention, and postponed their arguments until morning. Roderick settled to sleep but, tired as he was, it was slow in coming. His bruised body hurt wherever he lay and bright moonlight flickered in his eyes. Cries of owls and sinister rustles among the undergrowth, Diblin snoring and the incessant pangs of hunger in his stomach kept him awake. And Festy, curled at Janine's feet, yipped in his dreams. It must have been well after midnight before Roderick succumbed, and at the first crack of dawn Gwillym shook him awake.

He groaned as he crawled from the bedroll. His bruises had stiffened overnight and he was barely able to move, but the others were cloaked and hooded and ready to move on. Janine was among them. It was her life and her choice, she said, and the journey back across the ford to Woodholm was far too dangerous. So was the road to Dornaby, Roderick was informed. It ran through open countryside and their movements would be visible from every side. They would have to stick to the woods as far as possible. They would be heading eastwards, said Gwillym, making for Droon, a hundred and twenty miles away, which was the nearest town.

Roderick nodded dumbly, drank from the communal water flask and shouldered his backpack as best he was able, then set out with the rest of the group. A hundred-and-twenty-mile walk ahead of him – and nothing had been said about breakfast. Ice-cold water swilled in the hollow of his stomach. He felt light-headed and vaguely sick, but worse than that were the aches in his leg muscles and the throbbing pain in his arm and shoulder. Sunrise slanted through the trees, burnished the bracken and the yellowing leaves of oak, sparkled on grass and spiders' webs hung with dew, and dazzled his eyes. And almost immediately the others drew ahead, further and further, until he lost sight of them.

He was not unduly worried. The path was clear enough, a narrow grassy track meandering through the forest, and with the morning sunlight ahead of him he knew he was going in the right direction. A herd of deer fled through the trees at his approach and small birds twittered in the tree-tops. Red squirrels with tufted ears fed on acorns and beech nuts and chittered angrily as he came near. And as he walked, the advance of autumn grew gradually less pronounced, leaves on the trees retaining traces of greenness as if slowly, step by step, he was heading back through the seasons towards summer. Ripened blackberries in a sunlit clearing tempted him to stop and pick, and there were hazelnuts, too, growing in a thicket. He crammed his pockets, cracked them with his teeth and went on walking, leaving behind him a trail of broken shells.

The sun grew warm. He took off his cloak and thick woollen jacket, unbuttoned the homespun shirt and rolled up the sleeves. And the aches in his muscles eased as the morning wore on, as if his body adjusted to the exercise and the easy ambling pace he set himself. The path continued to twist and turn. Deer runs crossed it going in other directions and Roderick grew more and more confused. Once he heard voices, saw the pale dust-line of the road beyond the edge of the forest and a group of people travelling along it, pressed himself against a tree trunk and waited for them to pass. And on another occasion he found himself back in the Rillrush valley, its churning water glinting in the midday sun. The banks were lower here and he was desperately thirsty, but the path turned inland again, and the eyes of the water horse burned in his memory and he dared not stop to drink. But half an hour later he stopped for lunch: three flat breads, most of the cheese and two apples, which sustained him, at least for a while.

Late afternoon. The sunlight was behind him. Tree shadows lengthened and still Roderick was alone. His thoughts pitched towards panic. What if he had taken the wrong turning several hours ago? He could be lost in these woods for ever and no one would find him. It was all right for now, he could feed on nuts and blackberries, but when winter came he would starve. Maybe he ought to turn back? Or maybe he ought to shout for help and hope the others were within hearing distance?

And if they did hear they probably would not answer him, he thought. They had probably left him behind deliberately, glad to be rid of him. It was his fault they had dropped their original plans. If he had walked faster, and crossed the ford when they had, they might have been halfway to Dornaby by now. He was a liability, his weight and bulk holding everyone back – slower than an arthritic snail, Craig had said – and they would all be better off without him. Maybe he should do them a favour? Maybe he should head for the river and drown himself? They were not likely to escape the Grimthane while he was with them.

And he could not walk much further. The straps of the backpack hurt his shoulder, and his arm, where Craig had trodden on it, was virtually useless. He felt half dead anyway from thirst and hunger and exhaustion. Maybe, if he just lay down and slept, he would get hypothermia during the night and never wake up again? In which case he may as well stop right now, stay where he was, eat some more food and make himself comfortable.

He took off his backpack, buttoned the homespun shirt, pulling down the sleeves and put on his jacket to stave off the evening chill. He was about to unpack his bedroll and spread the shimmering cloak on the ground when the bracken rustled and a wolf appeared.

"Festy?" said Roderick in relief.

But maybe it was not Festy.

Its eyes glowed orange in the light, its lips

curled to expose its yellowed fangs, and it snarled menacingly. It was one thing to think about death, another to be confronted by it. Roderick snatched up the cloak and backpack and ran for his life. The wolf followed, trotted behind him at an ambling gait, its pink tongue lolling as if it laughed at his alarm. Thinking it had to be Festy, Roderick stopped. But its stance changed immediately. Again it snarled at him and again he ran, cloak and backpack clutched to his chest, his fat body being pushed to its limits. Then he was bound to stop and regain his breath, and the wolf seemed to understand. It waited until his breathing eased and his heartbeats steadied, then snarled again, darted towards him and nipped at his heels.

Running, stopping, running again, the miles passed swiftly and it was almost dark when Roderick reached the clearing. Low cheers greeted him. He saw the others sitting at their ease beneath an oak tree, their shimmering cloaks reflecting the last vestiges of sunset. And the wolf trotted past him, cocked its leg against a fallen log, then flopped on the grass between Carrie and Janine. It was Festy after all who had been sent to find him, round him up, drive him to where they waited. He saw the pale ovals of their faces, the white gash of their smiles, all of them amused by his plight. A huge anger rose inside him.

"That wasn't funny!" Roderick screeched.

"It got you here," Diblin said gruffly.

"It could have killed me!"

"Festy wouldn't hurt you," said Janine.

"Making me run like that!"

"It's part of the general keep-fit programme," said Craig.

"I could've had a heart attack or something!"

"But you didn't," said Carrie.

"And you are arriving with enough breath to speak," said Gwillym. "Now there's an improvement on yesterday, indeed it is. At this rate, in another few days, you will be setting the pace for the rest of us."

Roderick stared at them, and his anger turned to hatred but there was nothing he could say. They were all ganged up against him, even Janine, thinking they knew what was good for him and not caring how he felt. He sat on the grass, near them yet not near them, keeping himself separate and apart. His voice was sullen when he spoke.

"Are we staying here for the night or moving on?"

"We're staying here," said Gwillym.

"And we march at first light," Diblin said briskly.

Roderick nodded. That much established, he need never speak to them again. He undid the straps of his backpack, took out his bedroll and spread it on the ground. The others did likewise, preparing to sleep, but unlike him no one unwrapped their food parcels. They had already eaten, he supposed, and it would not have occurred to them to wait until he joined them. That kind of consideration was obviously beyond them. But as he tore off a chunk of flatbread he could feel them watching him. His mouth too dry to eat, he was bound to ask:

"Can I have some water, please?"

It was almost too dark to see, but Janine led him to a nearby stream and when he returned the others had confiscated his rations, left him with nothing more than half a flatbread and a pickled egg. He was accused of eating too much. Their supplies could not be replenished until they reached Droon and what they had with them had to last another six days, Gwillym informed him. One flatbread a day was the allowance.

"And you've already pigged three!" Carrie accused.

"Which means you don't have enough to last you," said Gwillym.

"And why should we have to share ours?" grumbled Craig.

"Best tighten your belt, lad," Diblin advised.

It was humiliating.

They'd had no right to go nosing in his backpack, and Janine did not offer to defend him. All over again Roderick hated them – or maybe hated himself? Keera's voice echoed in his brain. And he went to sleep hungry, awoke hungry, and was hungry all the next day.

Each day was the same. The weather varied through cloud and sunlight and rain, but Roderick was consumed by a hunger he could never forget. It was cruel and insatiable. He complained endlessly and the others snapped at him or gave him a wide berth. But more often than not he was alone, travelling through the forest at his own slow speed, the rest of them some distance ahead, although in the mornings, for the first mile or so, he managed to keep pace. Occasionally, one of them would be waiting where the woodland paths branched in different directions – Craig or Carrie deigning to keep him company for a while, chivvying him on with their snide remarks, or Janine or Gwillym or Diblin trudging beside him and trying to be pleasant. It was all a pretence. He knew what they thought of him, knew what he thought of them. And Festy, at twilight, was sent to guide him to the place where they were camped.

Gradually, over the days, the aches in his muscles disappeared and the terrible fatigue he had experienced was replaced by a healthy energy, but his hunger worsened. Festy hunted, fed on rabbits and woodcock and squirrels. But Roderick had nothing apart from a few mouthfuls of bread, a crumb of cheese, a portion of nuts and dried fruit, half a pickled egg a day and a couple of sour gherkins. He dreamed of beefburgers, roast dinners, bacon and eggs, boiled sponge puddings and custard. He dreamed of doughnuts, jam sandwiches, strawberry trifle and fish and chips. He dreamed of cooking what Festy caught – pheasant spit-roasted over an open fire.

"So why don't we?" he asked.

Gwillym shook his head. A fire might reveal their whereabouts, he said, and no one ate meat in Llandor unless they were forced to. Elves, dwarfs and humans were strictly vegetarians, except for an occasional marsh-eel stew or a grilled fish. And Diblin was even more adamant. Whosoever destroyed life and lusted for blood and flesh would be serving the Grimthane, the dwarf said darkly.

"We're all wearing goatskin boots," Craig pointed out.

"When animals die we take their skins," said Janine. "But we don't kill to get them. Leather is precious in Llandor, Craig. Most people wear clogs or rope sandals."

After that, Roderick kept his lust to himself. And when their supplies ran out, he lived on hazelnuts and blackberries, and edible toadstools Janine gathered from the forest. Too much raw food gave him a stomach upset, and there was no such thing as a toilet or wash basin or a change of clothes – no escape from his own bodily smells.

He was not the only one. They were all dirty and bedraggled, their hair unkempt, their clothes grimed with soil and grass-stains, creased and crumpled and smelling of sweat and sleep. Only the wolf stayed clean, its grey pelt groomed and sleek, scented by the woodland through which it passed.

Then, on the sixth day of walking, the landscape changed. The trees began to peter out, were replaced by scrub and patches of rushes. Gwillym had them stow away their concealing cloaks and take to the high road. There they mingled with other travellers who were heading eastwards, indistinguishable in their knitted jackets, brown homespun shirts and goatskin boots. Carters, tinkers and farm wives carrying cheeses, peddlers carrying their wares – everyone was making for the market in Droon. And they were, too, said Gwillym. They had come from the north, bringing leather goods and fabric for sale. But the town remained a day's walk ahead of them and they would stay that night in a wayside tavern. The prospect cheered Roderick enormously – a promise of hot food and a bath and a comfortable bed – and for the first time since they left Woodholm he began to enjoy himself.

It was a pleasant breezy day. Dust in the wind blew in his face and the Rillrush broadened, was joined by the Steepwash to become a sizeable river. Barren hills rose beyond it. And to the south was a land of dykes and stubble fields and withy beds, rutted tracks leading to isolated farmsteads and distant windmills, flat and level as far as the eye could see. Festy hunted vermin in a nearby ditch and the human traffic increased.

At first, after so many days of being by himself, Roderick found the presence of people strangely disorientating. The hubbub of voices made his head spin. Several times the crowd separated him from the others, except for Diblin who seemed similarly disorientated. The dwarf had never encountered large numbers of humans before, nor did he have any road sense. Twice that morning Roderick hauled him from the path of an oncoming cart, and a dozen times or more he had to shout at him to move aside. And each time Diblin swore or brandished a fist at whoever was driving, attracting people's attention.

"Who's your little friend?" someone asked Roderick.

"And where did you find him?" asked another.

Their questions left him floundering for a response. They were to say as little as possible about themselves, Gwillym had commanded. But again and again those in the crowd around Roderick wanted to know, especially about Diblin. Dwarfs, it seemed, were not commonly seen in that part of Llandor.

Roderick felt thankful when he caught up with the others. They were sitting on the grass by the roadside. Gwillym had exchanged a pair of goatskin gloves for cheese and a loaf of bread, a veritable feast which was shared between them. Cloud shadows chased across the land and late poppies bloomed and, to Roderick, no food had ever tasted so good.

Afterwards, back on the road again, the others slowed their pace and they stayed together. Diblin's safety was no longer entirely Roderick's responsibility.

"Keep to the flaming side!" Craig kept telling him. And eventually Diblin learnt.

The afternoon passed slowly with the miles. And sometime during it, Festy disappeared. There was still no sign of him when evening came, nor had he been seen by any of the other travellers heading for Droon. Janine worried, lingered on the roadside, called and whistled. He was probably off hunting, said Gwillym. And a wolf could look after itself, Diblin reminded her. He was sure to catch up with them, Carrie said consolingly. But Janine remained anxious. Roderick could sense it, although she hid what she felt, a fear of the Grimthane reasserting itself after days of forgetfulness. And the wolf was still missing when they reached the tavern.

It was a low rambling building with a thatched roof and rough plastered walls whitened with lime-wash. Across the yard at the back were other buildings, stables for oxen and horses, a shed containing bucket toilets, and a bath-house and laundry where water heated in a fire copper. Steam issued from the open door and Roderick gazed longingly inside.

Accommodation for the night – baths, laundry, breakfast in the morning, an evening meal and six tankards of mulled ale. Across the serving counter Gwillym and Diblin haggled with the innkeeper, as Janine and Roderick, Craig and Carrie sat at a table and waited. The room was already crowded, tables everywhere and rushes strewn on the floor crushed by people's feet. The ceiling was low with smoke-blackened beams. A fire burnt in the inglenook, and lighted oil lamps made soft pools of light. Serving girls in pinafores moved among the drinkers giving out stew and bread. And something from Diblin's pocket, that glinted like gold, changed hands across the counter top before Gwillym and the dwarf and six mugs of mulled ale finally joined them.

"That's us settled for the night," said Gwillym.

"Real beds!" cried Carrie in delight.

"And hot food," said Roderick.

"And a bath," said Janine. "And clean clothes to wear in the morning. Oh joy!"

Roderick sipped his ale in a moment of ecstasy.

"The man's a robber!" growled Diblin.

"In one way it's worth it," said Gwillym.

"A gold nugget...for one night?"

"Don't you have money in Llandor?" Craig asked curiously.

"To have money is requiring a banking system," said Gwillym. "But you can exchange goods for trade tokens in the major towns."

"The rest is open to barter," Diblin said crossly.

"Or given freely," said Janine.

"How positively prehistoric!" said Craig.

"And we've got nothing to barter with," Carrie said worriedly.

Gwillym smiled briefly.

"Keera gave us more than enough to pay for a passage down-river and a berth to Seers' Keep," he assured her. "And dwarfs are generally laden even though they are loath to part with it."

"We can't keep taking from you," Carrie objected.

"And what happens when we get to Seers' Keep?" asked Craig.

"Presumably the Seers will decide," said Gwillym. "They did with me. I do what I would have done anyway. So what are you interested in?"

"Computers," said Craig.

Gwillym frowned. "You're out of luck there, I'm afraid."

"In which case you can work for your keep like everyone else," muttered Diblin.

"Get a job, you mean?"

"A job?" said the dwarf. "What's that?"

"Working for wages," said Craig.

"Wages?" said Diblin.

"Money," said Craig.

"There isn't any money," Roderick reminded him.

"So what do people work for then?"

"Pleasure?" said Gwillym. "Meaning or purpose, maybe?"

"Or survival," said Janine.

"You mean you don't get any reward?"

"Surely the quality of life itself is the reward?"

"That's crazy!" said Craig.

"I think it's rather nice," said Carrie.

"If you want to grub around in a patch of earth for the rest of your life in order to survive then you're welcome," said Craig. "But it's not what I want to do. And it's not progress, is it?"

"Isn't it?" mused Gwillym.

"You should know!" Craig said pointedly.

"It depends what you mean by progress, see?"

"Tarmac roads, for one thing," said Craig. "Modern plumbing and decent toilets, for another."

"Asphalt and steam rollers," murmured Gwillym. "Sewage works and a public transport system. Televisions and washing machines and applied technology...that's what I thought once. But now I am not so sure. Better, perhaps, is a world where all people are fed and clad and housed, where there are no wars and no crime and no laws..."

"No laws?" said Craig.

"Where men and women are true and decent and honest, you have no need for laws, see?"

"So who governs?"

"No one," said Gwillym.

Craig gaped at him.

"Llandor's got no parliament? No king or queen? No warlords or generals? No governing body of any description?"

"There are village elders," said Janine.

"And town councils," said Gwillym.

"And we dwarfs choose a spokesperson," said Diblin.

"But no one sets themselves up," said Gwillym.

"We are all free people, Craig," Janine said earnestly. "If we look to anyone it is because they are wiser than we."

"Like the Seers," said Gwillym.

"Or Keera," Janine said softly.

She gazed at her tankard, her face momentarily sad. And Roderick wondered why she had done it, left Kern and Keera and Woodholm, given up everything she had ever had and all she held dear to make this journey. He was about to ask her when her gaze shifted to Gwillym and he understood. Janine was there for Gwillym but that could not be Diblin's motive.

Roderick's attention moved to the dwarf. Diblin, too, had sacrificed everything, left behind his mountain home, his way of life and all his kind, to accompany Craig, Carrie and Roderick to wherever they were going. He had even paid gold from his own pocket to provide them with food and shelter. In the world Roderick came from, people might give to charities, but very few would involve themselves in a personal way to their own cost. And what was he to Diblin? Or Craig? Or Carrie? What drove the dwarf to do as he did?

Roderick was about to ask when there was a sudden hush in the room around him, a cold draught from the doorway and everyone stared. Roderick saw alarm in Gwillym's eyes, disbelief in Janine's, and even Diblin looked shaken. Craig frowned, and Carrie's face whitened. Roderick quickly turned his head.

The man was tall and lean and cloaked in black. He carried a staff in one hand and a travel pack over his shoulder. A cowled hood hid his face. And a great grey wolf stood beside him, its yellow eyes gleaming in the lamplight. Roderick could sense a power about the man, something awesome and dangerous and impossible to define. People drew away from him, the atmosphere darkened, and the air seemed to crackle as he moved. Brown weatherbeaten fingers rapped on the counter top and the innkeeper scurried to serve him.

"A bed and a meal," said the stranger. "For me and my lupine companion. And a tankard of ale to be going on with."

In the room the hum of conversation began again, but softer than before, people whispering together and casting wary glances.

Janine leant across the table. "That's Festy!" she hissed.

"You will be daring to claim him?" murmured Gwillym.

"Who is that man?" asked Craig.

"Kadmon," said Gwillym.

"Otherwise known as the Wanderer," growled Diblin.

"Others call him the Black Mage," said Janine.

Whoever he was, his dark power chilled.

And Roderick saw Carrie shiver.

CHAPTER NINE

In the presence of the Black Mage, Carrie shivered. It was as if his darkness touched her deep inside, evoking a fear that was close to terror, although he paid no heed to her or to anyone. Then, suddenly, he turned his head and looked at her, as if he knew she watched him. His face in the lamplight seemed somehow timeless: hawk-nosed, thin-lipped, black-browed, with eyes that were dark and cruel as a predator about to strike, merciless eyes raking her heart and mind. Her terror rose. She felt helpless, paralysed as a rabbit caught by the headlights of a car, knowing she was about to die. And what she experienced seemed a kind of death – everything she was, and had been, erased in a single moment as she stared at him.

Then it was over. A feeling of calm washed through her, filled the whole room, and she was still and quiet within it, and so was he. The darkness of his eyes grew warm and gentle, sparkled with life and laughter, all the joy of a love she did not begin to understand. Very slightly, as if he acknowledged her, Kadmon the Wanderer inclined his head before turning his attention to other things – his payment for the innkeeper, a sigil of light marked in the air that shone eerily blue before it faded. Then he picked up the mug of foaming ale and, looking to neither right nor left, headed for the inglenook with Festy accompanying him.

A party of peddlers who occupied the high-backed settle moved elsewhere, not wanting his company. Abandoned within the space he had created, Kadmon was ignored. Conversations, interrupted by his arrival, began again and increased in volume, and business resumed as before. Only at the table where Carrie sat did the silence linger, each of them brooding on their own thoughts, bound to the wolf who bound them to Kadmon. Finally a serving girl brought them their meal of savoury stew and bread, and Gwillym shrugged.

"We'll have to accept it, I suppose."

"But Festy is ours!" Janine said tearfully.

"We cannot be owning a living thing that has its

own will, Janine. Free or ensorcelled, Festy has found himself another master, see?"

It was sad, thought Carrie, like losing a companion, losing a friend. On cold nights in the forest Festy's body had warmed her. And for Janine, the last link with Woodholm was broken with the wolf's defection. At the feet of Kadmon the Wanderer her wolf lay in allegiance as if it had never known her. And across the table, in Roderick's hazel eyes, Carrie saw a flicker of sympathy and a depth of understanding.

"I'm sorry," he said softly.

And she realized he meant it.

Later, she and Janine went to the bath-house, left their clothes to be washed and dried overnight. Scrubbed clean of everything except their memories, and dressed in loose hessian night robes, they re-entered the tavern by the back door and were shown to the room they would share. It was small and stuffy, high in the roof space with a tiny window overhung by thatch, and lit by the light of a single candle. The beds were pallets on the bare wooden floor, spread with linen sheets and a couple of blankets. There was no other furniture and they had to use their backpacks for pillows. Yet it was luxury after sleeping in the woods, and Janine saw no signs of fleas or bed-bugs, just death-watch beetles in the rafters and a cockroach that fled beneath the skirting board when she flung her boot at it.

They talked until they slept of all that was gone – Carrie's former world and former life, Janine's life at Woodholm, the years of her childhood and how she felt about Gwillym. It was because of Gwillym that Janine had left, Carrie learnt, although Keera had claimed he was a wanderer who would never settle.

"So I shall wander with him," Janine declared.

"And does he know you care about him?" asked Carrie.

"No more than Festy does," Janine said bitterly.

"Has Kadmon really cast a spell on him?" asked Carrie.

"As like as not," Janine said curtly.

"But who *is* Kadmon?" Carrie asked curiously. "Tell me about him, Janine."

The Black Mage, Carrie learnt, was an itinerant sorcerer, a harbinger of disaster. Bad things happened when he passed through – deaths, accidents, tempests, flash floods, family quarrels and disagreements between neighbours, people falling suddenly sick. He did not cause those things, exactly, but all the same they seemed to happen, and no one welcomed him or trusted him. And no one knew for sure what powers he possessed, but he could certainly lure away animals. And people, too, Janine said darkly.

"Why would he do that?" asked Carrie. "He must have a reason."

"Some say he's a servant of the Grimthane," said Janine.

"And is he?"

"Keera says not," Janine replied. "She met him once in Irriyan in the years before I was born. Kadmon belongs to no one. That's what she said."

"It must be true then," said Carrie.

"She's not always right," said Janine.

The candle burnt out, left only their voices talking on in the darkness. But eventually they slept until something caused Carrie to wake – a knocking at the door that Janine hastened to answer. Early morning sunlight filtered through the grimy window pane. Dust motes floated in the air. And one of the serving girls delivered their clothes from the laundry with a message from the landlord that breakfast was being served downstairs.

They dressed hurriedly in clean linen underwear, their homespun shirts and trousers newly ironed and faintly scented with lavender, and Carrie smoothed out the tangles of Janine's hair, plaited it tightly and ran her fingers through her own.

They would have to remember to buy a hairbrush in Droon, said Janine, as they joined the others in the main room of the tavern. Craig and

Roderick sat in the window bay, both of them heavy-eyed from lack of sleep, and Diblin was even more surly than usual. After days of comparative starvation, Roderick had overloaded his stomach with food and ale, spent half the night vomiting and kept them awake. Even Gwillym seemed dull and tired.

But Janine and Carrie had each other for company, a growing friendship forged by their gender as well as a week in the woods and the previous night's confidences. And there was no sign of Kadmon or Festy. Most people had left already, the innkeeper said, the Black Mage and his wolf among them.

Soon, after breakfasting on porridge and honey and herb tea, they too were back on the road again. An ox-cart laden with wattle trundled ahead of them and a horse-drawn caravan, which was home to a family of jugglers and acrobats, trundled behind. But the bright morning faded. The sky clouded and a cold drizzle came sweeping across the fenlands, increased after a while into drenching rain. The road churned to mud. Their thick knitted jackets grew sodden and heavy, but the shimmering cloaks that would have shielded them had to remain in their backpacks. Elven cloth could give them away, said Gwillym, and raise too many questions.

Craig tried to argue.

"Surely we're not still bothered about the Grimthane?"

"*You* may not be," growled Diblin.

"I've seen no signs of anything following us."

"And which are we to rely on?" asked Diblin. "Your eyes or my nose? I smell trouble, lad, even if you don't see it. I've been smelling it ever since last night. Where Kadmon the Wanderer goes there is always trouble."

"So we stay as we are," Gwillym said firmly.

And as they were, they were part of the crowd, just a group of ordinary travellers, supposed tradespeople on their way to Droon. Wetness seeped upwards through Carrie's boots, rain dripped from her hair, and passing carts splattered her with mud and water. Ditches by the roadside filled and overflowed.

They sheltered for a while in a village forge. The blacksmith was a half-dwarf, gruff and bearded. Huddled round his fire, they ate the meagre lunch of cheese and bread they had purchased from the tavern. Their clothes steamed and dried, but there was little point in lingering, and once on the road again they were as wet as ever.

Conditions were little better when they reached the town. Narrow cobbled streets and small paved alleys wound between tall buildings of timber and brick. Rain poured from the pantile roofs, swilled down the gullies, dripped from creepers that clambered over porches and trickled from the awnings of shops. And the stalls in the market square were already closing. It was too late to buy supplies or hire a passage down-river to Scupper's Key. The water was running high, almost in flood, murky with mud and debris, swiftly flowing, full of swirling currents and pitted by rain. The warehouses were mostly abandoned and the flat-bottomed barges lining the quays were empty of cargoes – none being loaded and none planning to leave. Not that evening, with the weather as it was, and probably not tomorrow either, they were informed. It seemed they would have to stay in Droon longer than they had anticipated, Gwillym said.

Accommodation was not easy to find. The taverns that lined the water front were heaving with stranded boat-people, every available room taken. In the tipping rain they must have walked a mile or more along the river road. Stone wharves gave way to wooden jetties. The moored boats were smaller – punts and skiffs and coracles – and the buildings grew meaner – shacks with tin chimneys and fenced-in vegetable gardens. Then, where the town ended in reed beds and rain-swept marshes, built on wooden stilts and protruding many metres out above the river, they reached the Boar's Head.

At that time of day, wet early evening, it was almost empty. Its lamps were unlit, but a pot-bellied stove filled the room with warmth, and food smells wafted from the kitchen. Perhaps they were in luck at last, said Gwillym. He knocked on the counter top and a plump landlady with an Irish accent came to attend them.

"Other-worlders!" she exclaimed in pleasure. "And newly arrived, at that. And haven't I been here twenty years or more without meeting a single one to ask what's going on at home!"

"We're travelling incognito," Gwillym informed her.

"Ah," said the landlady. "It's a spot of trouble you're in, is it? To be sure you're safe enough here. I recall what it is to be on the run – and not much more than a girl I was at the time. Still there, are they?"

"Who?" asked Gwillym.

"The Black-and-Tans," said the landlady.

"That was in 1922!" exclaimed Craig.

Once again Carrie was reminded of the difference in time between the two worlds. How long had she been in Llandor now, she wondered. Six months or more? Her life declared over? Her mother recovered from her grief and beginning to forget she had a younger daughter? The room blurred with sudden tears which she hastily wiped away.

And the landlady chattered on. There were vacant rooms a-plenty for as long as they were wanting them, she said, and as much food as they could be eating, but there were no laundry facilities and no bath-house. In these parts people were using the river. It was the seedy end of town but better than anything she had known back home in Ireland and she could lend them towels to dry themselves and the kitchen airer for their clothes. In this weather any shelter was better than none, thought Carrie, as Diblin reluctantly parted with another gold nugget.

She and Janine had a room at the front. Ill-fitting French windows opened on to a veranda that overhung the river and draughts whistled through the cracks in the floorboards. Wood lice and woodworm bred in the timbers, the bed-sheets were grey and unironed, and mosquitoes whined outside in the sodden twilight. They dried themselves as best they could, hung their heavy woollen jackets on the airer in the kitchen and returned to the main room to huddle round the stove and await the evening meal.

After a while Craig, Diblin and Gwillym joined them, but Roderick was feeling unwell and had gone to bed. The lights were lit, and the room seemed almost cosy, and at a table by the window three people sat talking in low voices. Carrie noticed them – a red-haired girl, dressed as Carrie herself was in brown homespun shirt and breeches, a young man with strangely pointed ears, hair as fair as Janine's and clothes which shimmered silvery in the light, and a man dressed in black who had his back to her. She might have thought no more about them, but then she noticed the wolf curled under the chair, its yellow unblinking eyes fixed on her face.

"Is that Festy?" she whispered.

Janine turned to look.

Her voice was loud and impulsive.

"Festy! What are *you* doing here?"

The wolf ignored her. But the three who sat at the table glanced round in response, the Black Mage among them. Again, within Carrie, came the lurch of fear as their eyes met, and the strange sweet aftermath of stillness. Then he dismissed her, nodded to his companions and rose to his feet. With Festy alongside him he strode past Carrie and the others and let himself out into the night. A magic sigil, left in the air, shone blue for a moment and slowly faded.

"Was that a coincidence?" asked Craig.

"Coincidence my foot!" growled Diblin.

"So what was he *doing* here?" Janine demanded angrily.

"Inquiring about you, cousin," the elf replied.

"Me?" said Janine.

"You and your companions," said the elf.

"Two youths and a girl, Gwillym the Mapper and a dwarf. He wished to know if you remained in Droon or had left already."

"And now he has his answer," said the red-haired girl.

"Should we be worried, do you think?" asked Craig.

They worried for a while but in the days that followed, while Roderick lay ill in the small back bedroom and fought for his life, they saw no more of the Black Mage and gradually forgot. It was a time of idleness and waiting, and Carrie came to know both the elf and the girl.

His name was Jerrimer, and his home the elven port of Avaron. He must have been born restless, he said, wanderlust in his soul that drove him to travel. On ketches and clippers he had worked with a crew of orcs, sailed round the coast of Llandor and met Maeve in a tavern in Scupper's Key. Maeve was the landlady's daughter, although she did not much like the tavern life. In her veins ran the mariner's blood of her missing father, a love of the river, a love of boats. She was as competent a sailor as Jerrimer, both of them plying their punts through the marshes, ferrying passengers or fishing.

They were lovers, Maeve confided, as she hurled her cast-off skirts and blouses in Janine and Carrie's direction, and sorted through her father's clothes for anything that might be suitable for Craig and Roderick and Gwillym. She shortened a pair of rat-skin pants for Diblin, too, although the dwarf remained unaware until later, unaware of anything or anyone except Roderick.

In a small back bedroom, reeking of coal-tar and herbal concoctions, Carrie sometimes took a turn at nursing. Roderick was no longer the fat objectionable boy she had known at Lydminster comprehensive, he was a human being, pale and ill, his gross body wasting away before her eyes. She overcame her previous reluctance to touch him, sponged away his sweat when she had to, held his hand during bouts of delirium, pummelled his back to bring up the phlegm and fed him gruel from a spoon when he began to recover. She realized she did not hate him any more, but pitied him instead, sensing he had suffered in ways she would probably never understand.

But she was always glad to escape from him, glad to hand over to someone else – to Janine, or Gwillym or Diblin, Maeve or her mother.

But usually it was Diblin. Hour after hour he kept watch beside Roderick's bed, and night after night he tended his needs, and many gold nuggets he parted with before Roderick was well enough to travel. It was a strange relationship – a surly dwarf caring for a human boy. But twice on the road, Diblin confessed, and unbeknown to anyone else, Roderick had saved his life – dragged him from the path of an oncoming cart.

"And that's what I owe him," said Diblin. "His life in return – not once but twice."

"It's the dwarven code of honour," Gwillym explained. Meanwhile, the spell of rain gave way to autumn sun. Migrating birds winged south across the marshes. Midges swarmed and feasted on any exposed flesh, and fleas and bed-bugs disturbed Carrie's sleep. Craig itched and was covered in spots, condemning the lack of hygiene and the appalling medical facilities, growing more and more angry as Roderick languished. He needed to be in hospital, needed an oxygen tent and antibiotics, according to Craig. But his concern ended with his words, Carrie noticed, and he did not offer to help in any way. He spent the days fishing and boating with Jerrimer, catching marsh-eels for the tavern kitchen and fresh-water prawns for sale in the town market.

They had a week of Indian summer and, towards the end of it, in a chair on the veranda with a blanket wrapped round his knees, Roderick sat in the sun and recuperated while Gwillym and the others made plans. They would leave the day after next. Maeve and Jerrimer agreed to ferry them down the river to Scupper's Key, a journey of several weeks, Jerrimer informed them. And Maeve's mother, for another gold nugget, would provide the supplies. It was bread and smoked fish she was offering, which was good enough for the rest of them, Diblin said, but Roderick needed fruit and yoghurt, light nourishing food to speed his recovery.

The next morning, carrying a basket and a shopping list and a length of shimmering cloth to exchange for trading tokens, Janine and Carrie went to the market in Droon. Mists veiled the marshes, but the river ran smooth in the sunlight, crowded with boats and barges heading in both directions, and the town itself sweltered in the unseasonable heat.

Last seen in the rain, Carrie had not much liked Droon, but it was different now...terracotta buildings of old, warm bricks, weathered timbers and quaint leaden windows, and pools of plum-coloured shade. Scarlet Virginia creepers clambered over the walls and a myriad smells assailed her senses – shops selling fish pies and tanned leather, perfumed soap and candles, dried herbs and hops, plum wine and pastries, lace and fabrics, pomanders and lavender bags, dried fruits and ripe apples. The reek of sewage was almost unnoticeable and vendors in the market square bawled out their wares. It was how towns used to be, she thought.

A sense of excitement gripped her, of history made present, something lost being regained – and a man with pale eyes seemed to be watching her. He was leaning against a brick pillar inside the exchange building, a peddler, perhaps, with sandy hair, regarding her intently. And his pale eyes narrowed as Janine spread the length of elven cloth on a trestle table and haggled over its value. He was gone when they left, but wandering round the market, clutching their trade tokens and making their purchases, Carrie saw him again.

He was standing in the entrance to an alley, and this time he was not alone. There was another man with him, both of them lurking in the shadows, staring at her and Janine and whispering together. Fear tightened her stomach and she clutched Janine's arm.

"We've got to get away from here," she hissed.

Janine gazed at her in alarm, glanced towards the men as Carrie rapidly explained. They were no longer in the entrance to the alley, but pushing their way through the crowds towards the girls. The man's pale eyes glittered determinedly, fastened on their faces and the other man had a scar on his left cheek.

"They're after us," Carrie said fearfully.

"They are not likely to do anything with all these people around," Janine decided.

"Suppose they follow us?"

"As long as we keep to the main streets..."

"What happens when we reach the river road?"

asked Carrie.

Janine frowned and nodded, dropped a hairbrush into the basket, paid with a token, then moved casually towards the nearest side street. Carrie followed her and the men followed them both. Then, when Janine gave the word, they began to run. But the side street, too, was crowded with people impeding their progress. They were pushed and jostled in all directions.

Cries of "Stop thief!" came from behind them, and hands reached out to grab Carrie's arm, clutched at her clothes, intending to hold her. The blouse she was wearing ripped at the seams as she tore herself free and sped with Janine down an empty alley. Their footsteps pounded the cobbles, echoed between the buildings as they ran, but sounds of pursuit were swifter still and when Carrie glanced behind she saw that the men were gaining.

"We're never going to make it!" she cried.

Janine entered another alley. Steep and flighted and dark with shadows, it led past the back doors of workshops and taverns in the direction of the river. Light on water glinted ahead of them. But the gap between them and their pursuers continued to close and Carrie was tiring, unable to run any faster. And even if they reached the river road it was over a mile to the Boar's Head. Nor, believing they were thieves, would anyone help them. They would be captured, both of them, and taken to a place where Gwillym would never find them.

Then, in a nearby doorway a darkness moved among the shadows, a man robed in black – and something streaked past them, grey and snarling.

"Festy!" cried Janine.

The men shrieked as the wolf attacked, and Carrie and Janine stopped running, turned to look. Light shone on a dagger held in a human hand that was dropped on the cobbles as the Black Mage struck. A blast of blue fire flashed through the air and the two men fled, returning the way they had come, with Festy behind them snapping at their heels. Kadmon lowered his staff. His black robes rustled and his fierce eyes flashed as he spun to face Janine and Carrie.

"Go!" he told them. "Go, and tell your companions to go. Leave this town now, today, before the Grimthane gathers his strength and you are still able. And next time peddle your elven cloth in some less public place!"

CHAPTER TEN

Droon faded in the distance behind them, although the road that passed the Boar's Head tavern remained visible, following the line of the river before curving away around the southern reaches of Sedge Marsh. For a while, after hearing of Kadmon's warning and not wanting to involve Maeve and Jerrimer in whatever dangers pursued them or lay ahead, Gwillym had been tempted to travel by road. But that way would have added several weeks and many more miles to their journey, and, according to Diblin, Roderick was not fit enough for a sustained march.

Finally, Gwillym had no choice but to confess the truth of their situation. Not only were Craig and Carrie and Roderick recent incomers to Llandor, he told Maeve and Jerrimer, they also had the Grimthane hunting them. What they needed was a boat in which to escape down river, which he and Craig would manage between them, and a navigational chart to show them the way. Maeve laughed. There were no charts, she said. And without direct knowledge of the waterways they would never find their way through Sedge Marsh, Jerrimer declared. He and Maeve would ferry them, as they had formerly agreed. They would take to the backwater channels where no one was likely to follow. And nothing Gwillym or anyone else could say would dissuade them. The punts were loaded, and by nightfall they were several miles down river.

Travelling with Craig and Gwillym in Maeve's punt, Carrie felt her fear gradually lessen, as if whatever threatened her had been left behind or the water itself provided a haven where nothing could reach them. The larger barges that followed would stick to the main channel, Maeve informed her, and the beast at the ford that had attacked Craig and Roderick must have been a kelpie. There had been kelpies in Ireland, she said. When she was younger her mother had told her stories about them. But there were none here in this part of the river. They only lived in clear, fast-flowing streams.

"Well, there's something to be thankful for," said Gwillym.

Later the air grew chill with a hint of frost. Roderick's cough echoed across the water from Jerrimer's punt. Frogs chorused among the reeds, and small birds roosted for the night. They lit the lanterns at stern and prow, frail pools of light reflecting before and aft. Lights on other boats made similar reflections, and for several hours the river traffic continued, the punts rocking gently as barges going in other directions poled silently past. Many tied up at jetties on the north shore, their crews spending the night at riverside taverns, but others travelled on, as did they, heedless of the cold and darkness.

The night grew eerie and still. A sickle moon hung above the southern marshes, and the reeds were silvered with starlight. Strange phosphorescences gleamed in the depths of the river.

To stave off the cold and the boredom of inaction, Craig relieved Maeve of the punting, and in the other craft Diblin took over. They had cold eel steaks and fruit for supper, and the river rocked them, and the same barge that had followed them from Droon followed them still.

When Carrie awoke at dawn, Maeve was sleeping with her head on Craig's shoulder and Gwillym heaved on the punt pole. Nothing else had changed. The landscape was the same as it had been yesterday, as if time and the river continued to flow, but they stayed motionless. She glanced behind, saw Jerrimer's punt caught in the same stillness...and the same barge quietly following. Her name, the *Bee's Knees*, was painted in white letters on her prow.

"Gwillym?" whispered Carrie.

"We know," said Gwillym.

"Can't we give it the slip?"

"We'll pull in later...see if it passes us."

"Suppose it doesn't?"

"Then we'll have to change our plans, won't we?"

To the south the reed beds awakened. The sound of frogs gave way to birdsong, and the low sun slanted in Carrie's eyes. On the northern shore the barren hills glowed red and gold as Maeve's hair, gorse and dead heather endowed with a brief beauty. They landed a few minutes later, scrambled ashore among sand and shingle and tussocks of grass. And the barge passed them, poled by a crew of four, laden with barrels of cider for trade at Scupper's Key, and leaving a pale wake on the surface of the river. Innocent after all, said Gwillym. But Diblin sniffed the air and frowned suspiciously, although he said nothing.

They stayed for maybe an hour, ate breakfast, washed and toiletted and stretched their legs before taking to the river again. They went ashore at nightfall, too, had grilled fish for supper, the same routine being repeated and setting a pattern for several days to come. Carrie began to enjoy the journey, except for the midges, and the moments when Craig reminded her of home. His discontent with Llandor, and the various comparisons he made with their former world disturbed an underlying sadness and a longing to return, set her in conflict with her own emotions.

"You're worse than Roderick used to be!" she complained.

"Always moaning," teased Maeve.

"Time to stop fighting and accept you are here," said Gwillym.

"I wouldn't mind if it wasn't so backward!" Craig retorted. "If we had a motor boat, instead of a punt, we could have been there by now."

"This way we remain in connection," said Gwillym.

"With what?" asked Craig.

"With the land and the river," said Maeve.

"That's important, is it?"

"It's a relationship we are losing where we were coming from," said Gwillym. "What do we learn of living things from fast boats, and aeroplanes, and bubble cars? It is the journey, not the arrival, that is mattering, see?"

"That may be your opinion," said Craig, "but the way I see it we're just wasting time. I mean, we're not doing anything constructive, are we?"

"How about nourishing our souls?" suggested Gwillym.

"Who says we've got souls?" asked Craig.

"Whether we have or no, what could we be doing that's better than this?" asked Maeve.

Nothing, thought Carrie. Apart from the occasional menace, their encounters with the goblins and the kelpie, their journey through Llandor seemed like an adventure holiday, an outward-bound experience that people would pay the earth for back home in Ditchford – strengthening their characters, testing their stamina, rendering them physically fitter than they had ever been before. She could feel it in herself, a power, and energy, an ability to endure. She could see it in Craig – the leanness of his body, the hardening of his muscles, his wiry strength. And laughter drifted across the water from Jerrimer's punt as a slender youth, who used to be fat Roderick, tried his hand at manoeuvring the craft downstream.

His was the most dramatic change of all. His cough had improved. His health was restored, his skin had cleared of spots. He was a different person, Carrie thought, a stranger she had hardly met and had not begun to know. And it was not just the land that gladdened Carrie's heart, but its people too, their friendliness, their willingness to help, Keera and Maeve's mother, the Black Mage also and the men and women who waved from passing boats. No trace of the Grimthane on the bustling river in the warm autumn days. Life was good, thought Carrie, provided you accepted it. And gradually Craig seemed to do so, found a temporary purpose punting and fishing, stopped complaining and appeared content. He even played ducks-and-drakes with Maeve and Janine at one of their stopping places.

It was the misty end of afternoon. The sun had grown huge and hazy, a great red ball sinking into the marshes. Stones from the pebble shore bounced across the surface of the water, rattled against the timber side of a barge heading for Droon. The *Bee's Knees* – Carrie read its name on the prow. It had not been to Scupper's Key at all, but had turned somewhere down-river, its cargo of cider barrels still intact. A trickle of fear ran through her and she was not the only one to recognize it. Jerrimer did, too, and so did Gwillym. And once again Diblin sniffed the air and frowned. They had an animal on board, he said, and something else as well, some familiar scent he could not quite name that boded trouble.

The need to escape returned to them. Before the barge could halt and turn again, they were back in the punts and on their way. And the mist thickened, rose from the reed beds and drifted like smoke above the water. Providential, murmured Gwillym. But it was also dangerous. River traffic passed as indistinct shadows, with only the lanterns marking their true whereabouts, but Maeve and Jerrimer took the risk of not lighting theirs. They were near to the place where the river turned southwards, where the north shore receded and they could slip away, take to the backwater channels where no barge could follow. Once within Sedge Marsh itself, they would be safe for the rest of the way, Maeve declared. And in readiness, they donned their shimmering cloaks for camouflage and kept their voices to a whisper.

Carrie did not notice when it happened but gradually the reed beds closed around her, a jungle of tall stems on either side. Sounds from the main river faded, were replaced by the muffled croaking of frogs. The pale mist drifted and shifted and the darkening water reflected nothing. This could be her world for weeks to come, reeds and water concealed by mist, the horizon narrowed to a scrap of sky above her head and no solid ground on which to set foot. From the face of Llandor, and the eyes of the Grimthane, and the barge that followed, they had effectively vanished.

Silent hours passed. Night gave way to morning but the mist remained. There was nothing to do and nothing to see but the reeds towering above their heads and roots rotting in the water – no sound but the occasional plop of a fish, the cry of a bird and their own whispered conversations. And there was a strange stagnant smell in the air, a reek of dampness and decay. It had an effect. Carrie grew chilled and depressed, full of lost, lonely feelings. Gwillym brooded on his own thoughts and Craig was tetchy. Only Maeve stayed cheerful, singing softly to herself as she propelled the punt unerringly on its way.

The day wore on, the smothering mist refusing to yield, with nothing to mark the grey uniform hours but the need of their bodies for food and drink and evacuation. With more than two weeks' journey ahead of them, they would be likely to die of boredom, Craig said morosely. But chuckles of laughter came from Jerrimer's punt and Maeve, forgetting her caution, raised her voice.

"Race you down the next stretch of water, elf man!"

"You don't stand a chance!" shouted Jerrimer.

It became a contest that involved them all. Laying aside their poles and using their hands as sculls, they pitted punt against punt, careering through the reeds. Wild duck fled with a rattle of wings, and the chill of stillness that had Carrie in its grip throughout the day changed to an exhilarating warmth. And the mist thinned at nightfall. A few pale stars and the thin rictus of the moon showed in the strip of sky above her head, and the reeds swayed gracefully with the slow movement of the water. In a moment of silence when the laughter finally ended, Carrie was touched by the peace of it all. Even Sedge Marsh could be beautiful, she thought. But then she heard the soft dip of an oar some distance behind.

She turned to look. The punts were close together, less than half a metre of water between them. She could hear Roderick breathing and her own heart thumping, see the shimmer of Janine's cloak, the shine of Diblin's eyes and Jerrimer's smile.

"Did you hear that?" asked Carrie.

"What?" asked Jerrimer.

"Someone's following."

"I never heard anything," said Janine.

"You must be imagining it," said Craig.

"Suppose she's not?" asked Roderick.

"It was probably an otter," said Gwillym.

"Do you smell anything, Diblin?" asked Maeve.

"Only the reek of the marsh," Diblin replied.

But their mood of levity changed after that. Sedge Marsh became threatening and they maintained a watchful silence. Small sounds unnerved them: rustlings in the reeds, the skitterings of water rats, cries of night birds and the sudden flutters of moths. Odd lights flickered and danced – will-o'-the-wisps, according to Jerrimer – but they might have been fires or lanterns. And once again, before she slept, Carrie thought she heard someone following.

At daybreak the mist returned, a great bank of it roiling across a stretch of open water. Blackmere, said Gwillym, fed by the River Crawdle that flowed from the north. It was dark with peat and unimaginably deep. Even at the edges the punt poles failed to find the bottom. With their flattened blades, Maeve and Jerrimer used them as single upright sculls and kept the reed beds well within sight. But the mist closed round them and they were caught in an undertow that swept them too far out. Instead of following the southern margins of the lake, they found themselves heading towards the northern shore.

Then the mist thinned. The horizons widened. Carrie could see the dry hills in the distance and feel the warmth of the sun on her face. And Sedge Marsh was not entirely waterlogged. Here and there were islands of firmer ground. On one, among a stand of tall willows, a colony of herons roosted. On another, willowherb seeded and osiers grew. And a third was inhabited. Stilt houses, thatched with reeds, overhung the water. Small wizened men fishing from coracles, women tending cook-fires on the shore, and stunted children playing on the small wooden jetties, paused and stared as the punts drew near. And a smell of roasting meat wafted towards them.

"Can we land?" asked Craig.

"Please let's," begged Carrie.

"It would be nice to stretch our legs," Roderick said wistfully.

"They might even feed us," Maeve said hopefully.

"We could certainly use a hot meal," said Gwillym.

"Roast eels," said Janine. "Or is it?"

Jerrimer's sharp eyes narrowed as he surveyed the village. And, balanced beside him, Diblin sniffed the air. Dwarf and elf regarded each other for a moment. Then the alarm showed on their faces.

"Do you smell what I see?" asked Jerrimer.

"Boggarts!" exclaimed Diblin.

"What *are* boggarts?" asked Craig.

"Akin to the goblin," growled Diblin.

"They eat meat," said Janine in disgust.

"Any kind of meat they can get their hands on!" said Maeve.

"You mean they could eat us?" asked Roderick.

"Let's get out of here," said Gwillym.

"Paddle!" urged Jerrimer. "Paddle for all you are worth if you want to stay alive!"

What had been a game before was now practised in earnest. They laid aside the poles and used their hands, clawing in unison at the icy water. But the punts moved sluggishly against the current and already a flotilla of coracles were in pursuit. Slowly the island slid past and they rounded a headland, made for the reed beds maybe half a mile distant, hoping to lose themselves among them.

The boggarts were gaining. Glancing back, Carrie could see the bald shine of their pates, their greeny eyes and pointed ears and otter-fur capes. They chittered excitedly. Some held barbed harpoons and were poised to throw, their fangs gleaming whitely as they smiled.

"We're not going to make it!" shrilled Carrie.

"Just keep paddling," Craig said savagely.

Maeve's red hair shone in the sunlight as she, too, glanced behind. "We're sitting ducks! Why don't they throw?" she asked.

"Maybe they want us alive?" said Gwillym.

"I don't understand."

"If they are under orders from the Grimthane—"

"You mean we might have a chance?" Maeve cupped her hands. "Fight them!" she screamed. "Fight them, Jerrimer! They're trying to take us alive!"

In Jerrimer's craft, Diblin drew his short-sword in readiness, and Roderick balanced in the stern gripping the punt-pole and preparing to swing. It was the last Carrie saw of them, poised for battle, as Maeve's punt glided into the reeds, travelling too fast to stop.

The waterway was narrow. They could grab the stems of sedge on either side and try to slow themselves down. Shrieks and chitterings could be heard behind them, Janine's cry of pain and Roderick's shout and Diblin's savage roar. The reeds made beads of blood on Carrie's hands, but it was not that hurt she felt.

"We've got to go back and help them!" she said.

"We could be killed if we do that!" Craig said viciously.

"But they want us alive, don't they?"

"Can we turn yet?" asked Gwillym.

"There's room up ahead," said Maeve.

The punt shot free of the reeds into a pool of dark water, but Maeve had no time to turn. Carrie shrieked as a monstrous head broke the surface. And the woman rose, her skin green as slime, duck-weed hanging from the soaked tresses of her hair. She was twice human height, wading through waist-high water towards them. Wrinkled breasts dangled almost to her waist. Her fingernails curved like talons as she reached for the punt. And others surfaced round her, a bevy of hideous daughters with aquamarine eyes, laughing as Maeve screamed at them, lashed out with the punt-pole in one last gesture of defiance.

Carrie hardly remembered what happened next. The craft was up-ended and she toppled backwards into the water, the others along with her. The punt-pole caught her stomach and winded her, and she came to the surface spluttering and gasping. She had a glimpse of sky, of Craig and Gwillym clinging to the reeds, of Maeve, small as a doll, clasped in the marshwoman's arms. Then came the howl of a wolf from behind her, Festy charging through the tangled reeds. They bent and parted and barely supported his weight, so that his rear end sank before he leapt again. But with yellow eyes blazing and fangs bared in readiness, Festy joined the attack. Just for a moment Carrie trod water, saw a figure wearing black robes in an approaching coracle, before she sank again in the weedy darkness.

Yet, somewhere above her, she saw and heard a flash of blue light, a snarl, a yelp, a human cry. And the air, when she rose, reeked of scorched flesh and burning hair. Nearby sedge exploded in a wall of flame, but her clothes were waterlogged and the sky blackened with her mind and, once again, the marsh dragged her down.

She did not know who saved her. Semi-conscious she was hauled from the mud, dragged through the reeds and laid on a dry shore. Voices called her. Hard hands pumped her back. She vomited vile water and sank into another darkness. How long it lasted she did not know. When she next opened her eyes she was being carried over someone's shoulder. Stones and scree slipped underfoot and her whole body was jolted and shaken. She was cold, shivering, and late afternoon shadows followed her up the slope. Dark smoke drifted across the marshes far below, and somewhere nearby Janine was weeping.

After a while, Kadmon unburdened her like a sack of potatoes, dumped her on the hard ground in the shelter of an overhanging rock. Dark eyes looked down on her from a face that was grim and unsmiling, raking her soul, before he turned to Janine. She was sitting on a boulder, as cold and shivering as Carrie was, her cheeks streaked with mud and tears. Round suck-marks of leeches showed on her skin, and marsh weed hung from the wet tangles of her hair. Wrapped round her left forearm, stained and filthy and soaked with blood, was a strip of material torn from one of Maeve's skirts, a tourniquet fastened above it.

"There is nothing you can do!" the Black Mage said harshly. "Nothing, do you hear me? The dead are dead, but you are alive, elf-girl. And if you would go on living you must do as I bid. The bite of the boggart contains a venom that can fester and kill. Give way to grief and lose your will to fight and not even my skills can save you. Now stay here. I will gather fuel for a fire then go to seek herbs that will heal your flesh."

Janine nodded dumbly and Kadmon turned on his heel and strode away, his sodden robes flapping in the dust-laden wind that whined across the upland plateau. To and fro he came and went, bringing furze and heather from the heights above them, laying a fire on a base of dry grass, and a store of fuel for his absence. Then he hunkered beside it and drew out a tinder box from a pouch at his belt. Blue sparks reflected in the fierce blackness of his eyes, and small flames licked among the grasses. He watched until he was satisfied, then picked up his staff and rose to his feet.

"Warm yourselves," he commanded. "And wait for me here. I will be as quick as I can."

Again Janine nodded.

And Carrie watched him go, a dark silhouette heading towards the sunset. A mile below, at the foot of the dry hills, the River Crawdle ran red as blood, reflecting the sky. Beyond it, Sedge Marsh stretched as far as she could see: reed beds and islands, channels of water, the open expanse of Blackmere, and pockets of rising mist – a cruel and deadly place. She could not bear to look on it and be reminded. She turned her back on it, held out her hands to the blazing fire. But the marsh remained and everything Carrie had lost was contained in Janine's hunched figure – her grief in the shine of tears that no word of Kadmon's could still. The loneliness appalled, separated them from each other, and made loathsome the land that Carrie had grown to love.

"Are we the only ones left?" she asked.

CHAPTER ELEVEN

It was not choice that kept Craig from sleeping, it was Jerrimer's crying and the memories of what had happened in Sedge Marsh. The scene replayed itself. They were nixies, Gwillym had told him later, water spirits, malevolent and evil. They had strangled Maeve and the wolf with their bare hands. And Craig had clung to the reeds – clung for his life, stricken by fear and unable to move –watching as Carrie almost drowned and Roderick killed the boggarts that had bitten Janine and harpooned Diblin.

If it had not been for Kadmon they might all have died. Blue fire streaked through Craig's mind. Sedge and the nixies burnt and the boggarts fled and still he had clung to the reeds and done nothing. It was not a computer game he could play again and hope to do better. It was something he would have to live with for the rest of his days – his own cowardice, his own failure.

He wrapped the elven cloak more tightly round himself. The fire had burnt low, and the night sky was spangled with stars. A chill wind blew from the north across the dry hills. St Elmo's fires flickered among the marshes below. The injured dwarf moaned in his sleep and Jerrimer keened along the river's edge, unrestrained and inconsolable, mourning Maeve's death. When Craig's grandmother had died, people had cried silently, his mother's eyes swimming with tears, and Janine had wept for the loss of Festy. But Jerrimer's grief was different, a wild incessant wailing out in the darkness that screwed Craig up completely.

He listened, and his feelings tore at him – rage and helplessness he was powerless to express. He did not know how the others could go on sleeping; Janine and Diblin, perhaps, drugged by pain and Kadmon's potions, but not Carrie and Roderick and Gwillym. He wanted to kick them into wakefulness, or scream at Jerrimer and make him stop. But beyond the fire the eyes of the Black Mage forbade him, dark and glittering beneath his hood, an intimidating power that caused Craig to hold his tongue.

He did not know what magic Kadmon possessed but he knew he was ruthless. He had seen him cut Janine's arm and drain her blood, burn the wound in Diblin's thigh before binding it with leaves and thongs of leather. He had seen him blast Festy's dead body to a pile of ash and bury Maeve beneath a cairn of stones, unmoved by grief. He had railed at them all, heedless of their despair. At his bidding Gwillym had salvaged what little remained of their belongings, Craig had hunted eels for supper and Roderick hauled fuel for the night. And again, at his bidding, they had lain themselves down on the hard ground and slept – all except Craig and Jerrimer who, in their separate ways, defied him.

"What troubles you, boy?"

Kadmon's voice, harsh as the wind, disturbed Craig's thoughts and demanded a response. And he may have owed his life to the Black Mage but he did not want to talk to him or provide the opening for an inquisition. He flung another branch of gorse on the fire. Flames crackled and Jerrimer's inhuman crying went on and on. But between Craig and Kadmon the question remained. What troubled him?

"Nothing," he said shortly.

"Nothing?" said Kadmon.

"Jerrimer," said Craig.

"Grief is natural, is it not?"

"Not that kind of grief. Not where I come from."

"Is it the emotion itself or the expression of the emotion that you find unacceptable?"

"I don't know," said Craig.

"Do you not feel grief yourself?"

"If I did," said Craig, "I wouldn't air it in public."

"If you do not express your feelings, then how can you release them or rise above them? And how can others know the truth of you? Understand or respect what you do not express? And how can they avoid adding to your hurt, or anger, or distress, or whatever it is you feel? Either by words or deed, are they not likely inadvertently to add salt to your wounds? And would you not hate them for doing so?"

Craig shrugged.

And the Black Mage leant forward.

"What seeds of ignorance do you bring to Llandor, Craig? What darkness formed in your own world festers within you? Or is it a gift you have brought that the Grimthane would use and unleash against us?"

Craig stared at him across the fire.

And his throat dried in sudden fear.

"How do you know it's me the Grimthane's after?"

Kadmon smiled and spread his hands.

"I don't," he admitted. "If I knew I would act. Your life for the peace of this land would be a small price to pay."

"Is that a threat?"

"A warning," said Kadmon. "From now on I shall be travelling with you. So look to the truth of your heart, boy, if you want to survive the journey."

Craig slept, finally, and when he awoke in the morning the fear of Kadmon was still within him. Sunlight shone brightly over the dry hills, the marshes below were wreathed in mist, and Jerrimer had gone, departed during the night and his grief along with him, although later he returned to follow them. But even without him the sadness remained, imprinted in their eyes and on their faces, in their strained expressions and their silences. No one spoke of Maeve's death, of Festy the wolf who had been their friend. No one spoke at all, in fact. They simply ate what Kadmon offered, fish baked in leaves among the ashes of the fire, and obeyed without comment when he ordered them to move on.

No one inquired where they were going, either. Maybe they no longer cared, thought Craig, or maybe they, too, were afraid of the Black Mage. He did not know and he did not ask. Remembering the previous night's warning, a death threat dark in his mind, he gave Kadmon a wide berth, lagged behind carrying the harpoon – extracted from Diblin's leg and once belonging to the boggarts. Ahead of him, Gwillym humped the single backpack retrieved from the marshes, and Carrie, pale from stress, with Janine beside her, red-eyed from weeping, trailed in the Wanderer's footsteps. Diblin, leaning on a rough wooden crutch and Roderick's arm, brought up the rear. Their rate of progress was as slow as the dwarf's limp; northwards over the hills following the line of the River Crawdle, northwards towards Mordican where the Grimthane dwelt.

A suspicion grew in Craig's mind that Kadmon had saved them only to betray them, but he did not voice it. No one, it seemed, was willing to question the leadership of the Black Mage, or even discuss it. And if anyone else noticed Jerrimer trailing behind, nothing was said, not even by Kadmon. The dour silence went on and on. And precious few miles they travelled before nightfall, and precious little they had to eat, just a single raw eel Gwillym had harpooned in the marshy margins of the river, a few tasteless rosehips and blackberries, and a sip of mead from Keera's flask.

There was no fire to cheer them before they slept. Fire would betray their whereabouts, Kadmon said. Again no one argued – and looking round at their dull, drawn faces, Craig realized that he did not know them any more. They were all locked up in their own thoughts and feelings, shutting him out – he had grown apart even from Carrie and Roderick.

The next day, surreptitiously, he watched them. They had lived in the same village, gone to the same schools, and now they were strangers, changed out of all recognition. Changed, he thought, in a way he had not, as if in some way they had left him behind. The sense of isolation scared him. He had no one to relate to any more. Even Gwillym seemed remote and indifferent, separated by a deadlock of silence that Craig did not know how to break.

Two days passed in the same manner, with Kadmon striding ahead, Craig and the others trailing behind him and Jerrimer following them through the unchanging landscape. The main expanse of the dry hills lay to the left of them and Sedge Marsh lay to the right with the River Crawdle winding between, murky with sludge. Freshwater streams were few and far between, but now and then they paused to slake their thirst, or rested briefly before travelling on, but mostly they walked, separately and together, up one hill and down the next, over the never-ending undulations.

Their elven cloaks billowed in the ceaseless wind. Dry grass and heather rattled around them. Gorse pods burst and shed their seeds and the only other life was rabbits and lapwings. By day the sunlight was harsh and cold, so that their faces grew sore, their lips chapped, their eyes watery. At night, sleeping rough by the river's edge or in a windswept hollow, they grew chilled to the marrow. There was never enough to eat, and all the while, as they walked, they had nothing to say to each other.

It was hard not to take it personally, thought Craig. Look to your heart, the Black Mage had advised him, and when he looked he saw a person whose former status counted for nothing any more. He was not who he had been at Lydminster comprehensive – a boy with potential and a good future ahead of him. He was a coward, a failure, someone who had frozen as others fought. Roderick had became a hero instead of him, saving lives while Craig saved only his own. It was a humiliating comparison, a seed of darkness that festered indeed, and he was uncomfortably aware of it until a black speck in the distant sky caused him to forget.

At that distance it was hard to be certain, yet somehow he knew it was a crow – a crow, dark as an omen, sailing on lazy wings down the spiralling currents of air, surveying the land below. There had been a crow in the woods, he remembered, before he and Carrie had encountered the goblins. And another in the Rillrush valley, shadowing Roderick on his way to the ford. He watched it suspiciously, saw others to the left and right of it, quartering the hills and the river and the edges of Sedge Marsh itself. They were searching, thought Craig. And who they were searching for he had no need to ask. His shout was louder than the booming wind, commanding even the Black Mage himself.

"Get down! Hide yourselves! Quickly! Quickly! Those crows are looking for us!"

Kadmon glanced back at him, and the others stopped walking, and twice Craig repeated himself before they understood. But on the open hillside there was nowhere to hide. He sensed their panic, knew they were about to run – movements that would be spotted from the sky in spite of their elven cloaks.

"Get down!" he repeated. "Cover yourselves with heather!"

"What about Jerrimer?" asked Carrie.

The elf was a long way behind, a moving shimmer on the far horizon, where no human voice could reach him. But something alerted him to the danger. The shimmer vanished and the hills were empty then, except for Craig himself. He crawled beneath a gorse bush, sat for what seemed like hours, the others nearby, unmoving, unspeaking, until the birds had gone and it was safe to emerge. Heads appeared above the heather. Kadmon arose and dusted his cloak. Roderick heaved Diblin to his feet, and Janine pulled the gorse prickles from Craig's clothes.

"That was well spotted, Craig," Kadmon said grimly.

"Did they see us?" Carrie asked worriedly.

"It's to be hoped not," muttered Gwillym.

Kadmon picked up his staff.

The day had changed and the sunlight was gone. Dark clouds piled to the north and a thin sleety rain began to fall, driven by the wind and stinging their faces.

"Whether they saw us or no, we need to find shelter," said Kadmon, "before the weather worsens. We should head for the river, I think." He led them down an incline towards a stream.

"Where is it we are going?" asked Gwillym.

"There's an overhang," said Kadmon. "I have sheltered there before in my wanderings."

"I mean where in the long run?" asked Gwillym.

"We head for the Moor Wife's cottage."

"Who's she?" asked Craig.

"My mother refers to her as Grandmother Holly," said Janine. "She is as old as the hills and wise. She will provide us with food and a place to recover."

"I've heard tell of her," muttered Diblin. "I've heard tell of where she lives, too. On the edge of Harrowing Moor!"

"Isn't that where the wraiths are?" asked Craig.

"Who told you of wraiths?" inquired Kadmon.

"I did," said Gwillym.

"So what *are* wraiths?" asked Roderick.

"Spectres," said Janine.

"Shades of the undead," echoed Diblin.

"They cling to the place where they lived," said Gwillym.

"You mean ghosts?" asked Carrie in alarm.

"As long as we travel by daylight, no ghost or ghoul will be abroad to see us," Kadmon assured her. "And no one will trouble us once we have gained the Moor Wife's cottage. Once on the moor itself we have only a few miles to cross before we reach her door."

But a lot could happen in a few miles, thought Craig. Even in a few minutes or a few seconds a lot could happen. They followed the stream and the gap between the hills narrowed to a chine. Water chuckled among the stones, tumbled in thin veils down miniature cascades, and the path to the river grew steep and treacherous. There was not enough room for two people to walk abreast, and Diblin's injured leg could not support him. With Roderick above and Craig below they were forced to carry him, slipping and skidding on the rain-soaked rocks.

Finally they reached a narrow beach of sand

beside the river, and the overhanging cliffs that would shelter them from the wind and weather. To the north an impenetrable tangle of withy and brambles and nettles, impeded any further progress along the river bank itself. Wet, cold and hungry, they sat with their backs against the sandstone wall, watching the rain sweep across the marshes opposite. After a while Jerrimer joined them, a silent presence sitting on a patch of shingle some distance away.

He was not the Jerrimer Craig had known and liked and fished with. He created an effect – destroyed the returning sense of companionship, inflicted an awkward silence. And he got to Craig, everything got to him – the rain, the silence, the enforced inactivity and Kadmon crouching like a clod of darkness brooding at the river.

"I'm getting sick of this," muttered Craig.

"You're not the only one," Janine replied.

"Well, there's not much we can do about it," said Roderick.

"What cannot be cured must be endured," murmured Gwillym.

"And a fat lot of help that is!" said Craig.

Water from the stream cascaded down the chine and chuckled across the sand. And the beach was littered with driftwood. There was no reason why they could not have a fire, thought Craig. In the murky onset of evening it was not likely to be seen and the thought of raw eel for supper again revolted him. He glanced at Kadmon huddled within the darkness of his cloak. He was afraid of him still, but not that afraid.

"We could have a fire!" he said loudly.

With a shrug, the Black Mage assented. And the very idea of a fire seemed cheering enough to rouse them from their torpor. Diblin, grey-faced from the pain in his leg, remained where he was but Craig and Carrie and Roderick collected driftwood, and Janine gathered the thin dry sticks that were strewn beneath the cliff. Gwillym borrowed Kadmon's tinderbox, and the small flames flickered. With a renewed sense of purpose, Craig took the harpoon and went hunting.

The cold rain soaked him and for maybe a mile he walked downstream, but the bank stayed sandy, unsuited to eels, and by nightfall he had caught nothing. But Kadmon, who fished by his own methods, had stunned several sizeable carp that were already cooking when Craig returned. Two-thirds of a fish each – it was enough to set their juices flowing but not enough to satisfy their hunger. Craig realized how Roderick must have felt in those long ago days when they first left Woodholm – light-headed, foul-tempered, and ravenous enough to want to eat what Festy killed.

He added wood to the fire. Wrapped in his

black cloak, Kadmon appeared to be sleeping and the injured dwarf muttered in his dreams. But there was no way Craig could sleep, not with Jerrimer sitting gaunt and wakeful in the nearby darkness, nor any of the others either. Light from the flames flickered on their unwashed faces – an insect crawled in Gwillym's beard, Roderick's hair was long and unkempt, wind – sores oozed on Carrie's cheeks and Janine winced with the throbbing pain in her arm. They were disgusting, all of them, thought Craig, and so was Llandor.

He raged silently within his mind, hated this land and all it had done to him. It had deprived him of any semblance of civilization, brought him down, forced him to run and live like an animal, half-starved, sleeping rough, enduring the stench of his unclean body and unclean clothes. It held terrors he had not even dreamt existed outside books and films and computer games – creatures of myth, evil and brutish – kelpies, nixies, goblins and boggarts that killed without conscience. Maeve, Festy and Benna were dead because of them; Janine and Diblin injured and Jerrimer stricken with grief and madness. And still such creatures were allowed to exist – the ungoverned people of Llandor going about their business and doing nothing.

"It shouldn't be allowed!" he said angrily.

"What shouldn't?" asked Janine.

"What happened back there," said Craig. "It shouldn't be allowed!"

"It was hardly preventable," said Roderick.

"Then it ought to be preventable!" Craig said hotly.

"By what means?" Gwillym asked him.

"With a bit of organization you could wipe those creatures out!"

"I could live in a world without boggarts," muttered Janine.

Jerrimer raised his head. "And in a world without nixies, Maeve wouldn't have..."

It was the first time the elf had spoken since Maeve had died.

His voice, choked with emotion, failed to finish the sentence, but Craig knew what he meant. They all knew.

"Quite!" Craig said brutally. "In a world without nixies, Maeve wouldn't have died. So why haven't they been exterminated?"

"All things have a right to live," said Gwillym.

"And we've exterminated enough species on Earth without doing it here!" Carrie said fiercely. "There aren't many wild animals left on Earth outside game reserves! And we may not like what nixies are but they're bound to have a purpose, otherwise they wouldn't exist in the first place!"

"Normally," said Gwillym, "they feed on marsh eels. There are eels thirty feet long in Sedge

Marsh, see? Without nixies and boggarts, Llandor would be overrun."

"In that case you need to drain the marshes," said Craig.

"That's destroying a natural habitat," said Carrie.

"Who comes first?" asked Craig. "Nixies and boggarts? Or human beings? There's thousands of square miles out there which could be turned into useful agricultural land where people can live."

"And what about the birds and flowers and butterflies?"

"They can move elsewhere."

"Elsewhere and elsewhere until there's nowhere left!" Carrie said wildly. "Beautiful things, gone for ever! We've done that, too, on Earth! And then you'll trawl the oceans to get rid of sharks – kill the coral reefs, the dolphins and angel fish! And fire the forests to get rid of wolves and bears. Festy was a wolf, Craig! Festy was a killer! That was his nature! Maybe it's the nature of nixies and boggarts, too? They are what they are and so are we, except that we have a choice! We can choose to allow other things and other creatures to exist besides ourselves! We can choose not to kill them and not to destroy the places where they live! Isn't that what *makes* us human beings?"

Craig stared at her in silence.

They had been friends once, he and Carrie, but she had turned against him and the nearby darkness stirred where Kadmon sat and listened. Craig remembered then – his life was a small price to pay for the peace of Llandor. Rampaging nixies apart, if Kadmon's idea of peace was to have things remain as they were then he, Craig, had better mind what he said.

"OK, I'm wrong," he admitted.

"You were a bit over the top," said Gwillym.

"I know one thing," Roderick said quietly. "No animal or person is going to die because of me, not ever again."

Craig grinned nastily.

"So how did it feel to kill a boggart?" he asked. "Or was it six? Next time one of us gets harpooned by something you'd better think twice before smashing its brains in – Lady Greenpeace mightn't like it."

CHAPTER TWELVE

It snowed in the night, a faint white covering over the hills.

The sky was leaden grey and the wind, still blowing from the north, chilled Craig to the bone. He could see, in the distance beyond Sedge Marsh, other hills that marked the edge of Harrowing Moor, but there was no way they would reach the Moor Wife's cottage before nightfall, not if they stayed together. The dwarf's limp had worsened, slowing their pace, and he and Roderick fell further and further behind as the others froze and waited. They had lost their woollen jackets in the marsh, along with their backpacks, and had nothing but the thin elven cloaks to protect them. Janine's lips turned blue, and her arm festered along with her thoughts.

"This is a ridiculous situation!" she muttered.

"What is?" asked Gwillym.

"What is the point of dying of cold and starvation waiting for Roderick and Diblin?"

"*Are* you dying?" Kadmon asked sharply.

"I shall be if I stand here much longer," said Janine.

"So you would have us leave them?"

"Our waiting does not help them!" Janine said defiantly. "They will get to the Moor Wife's cottage eventually whether we are with them or not!"

"Then go, if those are your feelings!" the Black Mage told her.

"All right, I will!"

Janine tossed her head and strode away. And after a moment, Craig followed. He had been noticing it all morning, the subtle changes of allegiance – Carrie choosing to walk beside Kadmon, Gwillym and Jerrimer seemingly together, while he and Janine became somehow isolated. He supposed it had something to do with the conversation the night before and the attitude he had taken, but he could not remember Janine playing much of a part. She was half-elf, in tune with the land. She might be upset about Maeve and Festy's death, but she would hardly turn against Llandor or wish to change it. He drew alongside her.

"Janine?"

"What?" she said crossly.

"This isn't like you."

"Why isn't it?"

"It's Roderick and Diblin back there."

"Do *you* want to hang around waiting for them?"

"No," said Craig.

"Well then," said Janine.

It was the end of the argument as far as she was concerned. Her blue eyes were fixed determinedly on the distant hills, and the fair tangles of her hair streamed out behind her in the wind. Craig had almost to run to keep pace. The exercise warmed him, brought his cold limbs back to life and sent a renewed flow of energy coursing through his body. Yet he could not help feeling that something was wrong. Not with him – it would have been all right if he had lost patience and gone storming off – but it was not right for Janine.

"Can we slow down?" he asked.

"If you wish to slow down then you can wait for *them*!"

"So what's the sudden hurry?"

"You can ask? Haven't you had enough, too? Haven't we all? I am not sleeping another night out on these hills! I want a bath and a bed and a proper meal! I want to feel safe again and stop running. I shall be all right once we reach Grandmother Holly's. I shall feel differently then. But I can't think about *them* any more. I can only think about *me*."

Craig glanced back. The others were small specks on the horizon, indistinguishable from each other and without identity, as if the land and the sky were about to swallow them up, leaving only himself and Janine. And what loss would they be to him? he wondered. How much would he care? He liked Gwillym well enough but Kadmon scared him, and Carrie opposed him and he and Roderick had never been friends; Diblin he had never got to know and the comradeship that had once existed between him and Jerrimer had died with Maeve. In truth Craig had no ties left with any of them, not any more, and whether they caught up with him or not, or whether they went their separate ways, did not really matter. He wished them well, of course, but Janine's company was as good as any, and to reach the Moor Wife's cottage by nightfall provided them with a mutual purpose. The others could take care of themselves, thought Craig.

Immediately his mind felt lighter, as if he had made a choice. Heads bent against the wind, he and Janine hastened on, companions in adversity, separated from the others and heading for the same destination.

"It's like we've escaped from something," said Craig. "Jerrimer's mournfulness, for a start."

"Elves seldom witness death," said Janine. "Their lives are many centuries long and when the end approaches they sail from Irriyan to the Isles of the Blessed beyond the western ocean. To an elf, death is not a cessation of life but a departure – so Jerrimer does not know how to bear what happened to Maeve."

"Is that what you believe?" asked Craig.

"About Jerrimer?" asked Janine.

"About death," said Craig.

"I would rather talk about life."

"You're right," said Craig. "Let's talk about life. Let's talk about here and now and how glad I am to be with you, Janine."

She smiled and tucked her arm through his.

"If not for you I would not have come on this journey at all," she said. "I would still be at Woodholm with Kern and Keera, a child compared to what I am now."

"What about Gwillym?" asked Craig.

"What about him?" Janine asked indifferently.

"Gone off him, have you?"

"What do you mean by that?" she demanded.

"I thought it was for him that you came with us."

"I suppose Carrie told you that!"

"I guessed," lied Craig.

"Then you guessed wrong!" Janine announced. "Did I?"

Craig smiled. That Janine had gone off Gwillym was no bad thing. She deserved better than a footloose hippie, a man who was going nowhere and hardly noticed she existed. "How's your arm?" he inquired.

"It's not hurting at the moment," she said.

"It wouldn't have hurt at all if you'd had a shot of antibiotics," Craig informed her.

She looked at him curiously. "Tell me about your world," she said. "It's obviously changed since my father lived there. Could you really drain those awful marshes? Rid Llandor of its evils? Tell me about it, Craig. I would like to understand."

"If we were there," said Craig, "we'd be walking along a tarmac road, hitching a lift on a passing truck and stopping at the first motorway service station for a hamburger and chips."

"What is chips?" asked Janine. "What is tarmac? And what is a truck and a motorway service station and a hamburger? If you dream of those things for Llandor – and you want me to share that dream – you will have to explain."

It was not easy. Explaining a mechanized and technological society to someone who had no idea of it, was like trying to describe colours to a person who was blind. Janine could not imagine light at the flick of a switch, pylons and power stations and central heating systems, or hot water flowing from taps. She could not imagine Lydminster at night with cars and traffic lights, neon signs and fast-food restaurants, a five-screen cinema, a leisure centre and a skating rink. Or modern housing estates where everyone owned a television and a washing machine, had fitted carpets, refrigerators and matching bathroom suites. She knew nothing about aerodynamics, radio transmission or computer science.

Craig did his best; talked as the miles passed behind them, as sleet blew in their faces and washed the hills clean of snow. And dimly Janine began to understand. Llandor was primitive and impoverished in comparison with the world Craig knew and, for all their longevity, human beings had made no progress there.

"You can't really progress as a nation without some kind of organizing principle," said Craig. "I mean, nobody likes governments very much but they are necessary."

"What is a nation?" asked Janine.

"Don't you even know that?"

"No. Why should I?"

Craig shook his head in mock despair.

"It's people of the same descent living in the same land," he said. "The humans of Llandor are a nation and the elves in Irriyan are another; and the dwarfs are another – or they could be if they thought of themselves that way. Again you need an organizing principle, a monarchy or a republic, some unitary form of government. Usually the people of a nation work together for their own betterment: better roads, better housing, better sanitary conditions, better education, better medical facilities, a better standard of living for everyone, in fact. That's what we mean by progress."

"And in Llandor there is none," murmured Janine.

"Obviously not," said Craig. "It's unchanging, isn't it? A non-progressive society. Windmills and watermills, hand looms and spinning wheels, are all very well, but it takes a very long time for a bag of flour or a length of cloth to reach the market. If things were mechanized you could produce a hundred times more in a tenth of the time, which would increase your income as well as your leisure, and feed and clothe a hundred people instead of one. In other words, you could work less and have more. And that has to make sense, doesn't it?"

"I suppose it does," Janine admitted.

"I don't understand why it hasn't already happened," mused Craig. "I mean, the human beings in Llandor originally came from the same world I come from and, presumably, share the same basic instincts, so how come they're still living like peasants? It's odd, isn't it? Why isn't there any form of leadership? And why hasn't there been an industrial revolution?"

"Maybe they like things as they are?" Janine suggested.

"I can't believe that," said Craig. "Who really wants to hump water from a well to fill a copper? Saw wood, clear ashes, rekindle a fire, then wait hours just to have a bath or wash a few clothes? Who wants to walk through the rain for days on end along muddied roads to reach the market? Where's the stagecoach that preceded the modern public transport system? Why hasn't the steam engine been invented? It's almost as if there's some kind of repressive force."

He paused on the edge of an idea.

Before him, beyond the valley of the River Crawdle, the hills of Harrowing Moor rose stark and intimidating in the late afternoon, bitten grass and rocky crags, cold and inhospitable. It was a landscape similar to the mountains of Wales where Gwillym would feel at home, a place that Carrie would admire as another natural habitat, a haven for rabbits and eagles and a few tattered sheep. But it offered nothing to Craig and nothing to the people of Llandor in general, except its potential as an untapped source of metallic elements and hydro-electricity. And what stopped them? he wondered. What prevented them reaping the wealth of the land and their own intelligence?

"Tell me again about the Grimthane," he said.

Janine stared at him, and her face grew pale.

"Tell me," he commanded.

"He is the Evil One," she whispered.

" 'A hunter of souls who searches for his own reflection'," quoted Craig. "'All men serve him who serve their own base natures and uncontrolled desires'. And everyone in Llandor is afraid of him, right? Afraid to desire anything at all for fear of serving him. But if you don't desire anything, then you don't do anything because you have no motive, so everything stays as it is. And of course there's no government here – the Grimthane rules anyway, by his very existence. Anti-life, anti-progression, no wonder he's after us! We're dangerous!"

"What are you saying?" asked Janine.

Craig turned to her.

"Inside ourselves we all run, we all hide – you said that, Janine. But me and Carrie and Roderick come from another world. We bring new thoughts and new ideas. If we don't submit to the status quo, if we don't accept what is and cease to question, then we're dangerous. We could infect people, stir things up, start a revolution. Somehow or other we've got to be stopped. So we're hunted – hounded – until we comply. It's happening already, isn't it? Roderick and Carrie are turning native, forgetting where they came from and beginning to accept. The peace of Llandor...the backwardness...it's synonymous. And my life is a small price to pay for keeping things as they are. He actually told me that!"

"Who did?" asked Janine.

"Kadmon," said Craig. "And whose side is he on?"

Her blue eyes widened.

"But Kadmon saved our lives, Craig! In Droon he saved me and Carrie from the clutches of those men, and in Sedge Marsh he saved us all from the nixies. We would be dead if not for him! Why would he do that if he serves the Grimthane? And Gwillym came from your world, too. Why hasn't he been hounded these past three years?"

Craig shook his head.

"Gwillym's no threat," he said. "He's a love and peace man, a genuine nineteen sixties hippie, the Grimthane's unknowing tool. There's no way he'd rock the boat. I'm the only one left, Janine! The only one who poses any real threat. It's me the Grimthane is after!"

The realization appalled him and his isolation grew complete. In that wild rain-drenched land he had nowhere to hide, no one to help him, except Janine, and he was not yet sure about her. Maybe he would never be sure. She tugged his sleeve.

"We must go," she said urgently.

"Go where?" he asked.

"To the Moor Wife's cottage. Grandmother Holly will help us. She will know what to do. And if Kadmon is servant of the Grimthane, she will know that, too, and bar the door against him."

Craig hesitated.

"You think you can trust her? A person you've never met?"

"I think I can trust my mother," Janine replied.

Through the murky end of afternoon they hastened on. And the bleak high hills of Harrowing Moor grew nearer. Then, suddenly, they were no longer walking through grass and gorse and heather, but on a paved road, or what remained of it. Who built it Janine did not know, nor did she know who built the bridge that arched across the River Crawdle. It was a single slender span supported on stone buttresses, fifty metres high, rising from the gorge below them. Huge granite blocks with bevelled edges fitted so accurately together that not even a knife blade could be pushed between them. It was a spectacular piece of architecture, finer than anything Craig had seen since he came to Llandor.

And once on to the moor itself, what he had thought to be crags topping the hills were clearly the ruins of gigantic buildings, of a former civilization more advanced than any that existed now.

He saw fallen walls above him containing

arches of windows and gaps of doors, fragments of stairways leading upwards into nowhere, tumbled flagstones that might once have been a floor, conduits for heating, and broken drains. And the wind mourned eerily around the heights, whined in the gathering twilight, wailed and cried like dozens of melancholy voices.

Giants, was it? Giants had built the Trineway, Craig remembered Gwillym telling him. But there were no giants now in Llandor. What had happened to them? he wondered. Where had they gone? And what remained to haunt the place they had lived? Vague translucent shapes moved through the twilight towards him.

"Janine?" Craig said fearfully.

"The wraiths can't hurt you," the elf-girl replied.

She kept to the foot of the hills and Craig followed, his footsteps sinking in an ooze of moss and grass. It was almost too dark to see. The vast expanse of Sedge Marsh stretching away to the right of them was more an awareness than an actual perception. Craig just knew it was there, that all it needed was a moment of panic or a slight deviation in direction and it would suck him down to his death. Its pale fires fluttered as if to lure him towards them. Rain blurred his vision and the voices in the wind pursued him, sobbing, crying, mourning, unbearably sad.

Jerrimer's grief was nothing compared to this.

"Janine?"

"They can't hurt you!" she repeated.

"But what are they? What were they?"

"I don't know what they were," Janine said grimly. "But I know what they are now. They're dead, Craig. And we're alive. So pay no heed to them."

"I think something terrible must have happened to them," Craig murmured. "They're trying to tell us—"

"Don't listen to them, Craig!"

Her voice was angry. She gripped his arm, tugged him along. And all the while the wraiths were singing in his head. He needed to stop and listen, needed to understand what they were saying. They wanted him to know...wanted him...he could feel them at his back, invisible hands reaching out towards him, touching, imploring – the dead needing the living as Janine pulled at him, screamed at him.

"They're dead! They're dead! There's nothing you can do for them! No way you can help them! Don't listen to them, Craig! Don't listen!"

Her voice was harsh and compelling, a girl in the darkness, wanting him to go with her. But the wraiths sang sweeter than she, their wild unearthly song drowning his mind in sadness. His footsteps lagged and their singing rose to a crescendo. Then the night turned wild and mad around him. Things honked and cackled...white things coming towards him...pale snake-like necks...a flutter of wings. He clapped his hands over his ears and howled in sudden terror.

"Help me, Janine!"

Pain pierced his senses.

Something pecked his thigh and Janine shook him.

"They're geese, Craig! They're Grandmother Holly's geese! We're nearly there! Nearly at the Moor Wife's cottage! So move, will you! Move before the wraiths come back!"

He had no choice. He had lost the will to resist and she had hold of his arm, the clinging of her fingers strong as a vice and hauling him with her, the geese honking at his heels. He felt strange and bewildered, and his face was wet with rain or tears, although he did not know why he should be crying. He saw the outlines of hills towering above him, crags against the sky, and a white paling fence nearby, a wicket gate that led into a garden in a valley. But something reminded him, something infinitely sad and barely remembered. He turned to look back...and the geese waddled away as Janine opened the gate and ushered him through.

Then he forgot. The very air seemed to change, as if he had crossed an invisible barrier, escaped from death back to life. The rain felt warmer, almost springlike. He could smell flowers, and earth, and sap, and green things growing. Trees rustled their branches and there was a light in a downstairs window somewhere ahead, reflections on a flagstone path as he and Janine approached, and a waft of smoke from the cottage chimney.

She knocked at the door.

"What happened back there?" he asked her.

"Don't you remember?"

"If I did I wouldn't ask."

"I am not sure I can tell you."

"It wasn't just geese, was it?"

"No," said Janine. "It was the wraiths' song, Craig, but your experience of it was not mine. It obviously affected you in some way. Took over your mind, perhaps? But you can forget about it now. We shall be safe inside in another few moments."

There was a sound of bolts being drawn back, the turn of a key in the lock, and the door opened, letting out the light and warmth and a smell of cooking. Janine stepped forward.

"Can we come in, Grandmother Holly?"

"Daughter of Keera!" an old voice replied. "Come in indeed. And come in the boy who is with you. Umla and I have been expecting you for several days."

The room was small and bright. Gay curtains

hung at the leaden windows and lanterns, hanging from the black-beamed ceiling, cast a mellow light. There were rag rugs on the floor, patchwork cushions on the settle, a bowl of late chrysanthemums on a polished table. And a fire burnt in the open hearth where a hunch-backed child sat on a stool among the ashes, stirring the contents of a blackened saucepan. Craig could not see her face, just a tuft of hair tied with a scarlet ribbon on top of her head, a blue dress and scrawny arms and grey scaly skin – one deformed glimpse and the delicious scent of stew, before he turned to make the acquaintance of the Moor Wife.

She was a tiny, shrunken woman, so frail the wind could have blown her away. Her hair was white, her face creased with wrinkles, her hands gnarled, her legs thin as sticks beneath a grey voluminous skirt and starched white apron. Yet there was a strength about her too, an indomitable power of life, and her eyes were sharp as scalpels, missing nothing. Old and wise, Janine had said of her, but she was more than that. Meeting her gaze, Craig felt that she knew him in a way that he did not even know himself.

"This is Craig," said Janine.

The old woman favoured him with a nod of her head.

"Where are the others?" she asked.

"We came on ahead," Janine explained.

"Indeed you did," the Moor Wife said. "I heard the wraiths a-clamouring after you and smelt the boggart bite a-festering more than a league away. A stench of darkness, girl. It hangs about both of you."

"We have to talk to you, Grandmother Holly."

"Talk can wait," the old woman said. "Where time is no time we can talk for ever, but first things first. Sit you down with Umla, and warm yourselves beside the fire. I will bring you milk and bread to eat and brew you a tea that will heal both your hearts and your heads. Never you fear, my dears. You will be safe from yourselves and the Grimthane in Grandmother Holly's keeping."

Toothless gums glistened when she smiled, and Craig did fear. He feared the Moor Wife even more than he feared Kadmon – feared what she was and what she knew. She was no dear, sweet, apple-cheeked old lady; she was another one of Llandor's horrors. His voice was a hiss when she hobbled from the room.

"Don't tell her!" he said.

"Don't tell her what?" whispered Janine.

"Don't tell her anything of what we talked about! Don't tell her anything at all! Just keep it buttoned, right?"

And the child at the cooking pot turned her head. Huge milky white eyes regarded Craig, and her grin exposed a set of sharp pointed incisors. She stabbed a fork in the pot and held it towards him – meat cooked with herbs, the leg of a rabbit, food forbidden in Llandor, delicious and tempting. And this was Umla, not a child at all, not even human, but a goblin.

CHAPTER THIRTEEN

The morning was bright and cold, yesterday's rain frozen to ice and the hills clad in hoar frost, sparkling in the sunlight. The wind had eased and the past night, spent huddled together for warmth in a stony gully, was best forgotten. In spite of his hunger, Roderick felt unusually cheerful, and it seemed they all did, apart from Jerrimer. There was a lightness in their steps, animation in their voices, a shared sense of relief as they neared the end of the present stage of their journey. Even Diblin was somewhat improved, hobbling along with only the crutch to support him and refusing Roderick's assistance.

The grey-green hills of Harrowing Moor grew ever nearer, dotted with sheep and topped with towering crags. They reminded Gwillym of Dartmoor; high tors and rocky outcrops resembling walls and turrets, the remains of medieval castles or the homes of giants. And that, said Kadmon, was exactly what they were.

"Castles?" said Gwillym.

"The homes of giants," the Black Mage replied.

"There were giants living on Earth, once, according to the Bible," said Carrie. "But they've gone, too, except in fairy tales."

"What happened to them?" asked Roderick.

"A war," Kadmon said grimly.

Roderick found it hard to imagine a war taking place in Llandor. It was not like Earth, disparate nations squabbling over territorial boundaries or religious beliefs. But once upon a time, said Kadmon, the whole of Llandor had been ruled by giants. The ruins of their race were everywhere, although time had dimmed the memory of their downfall.

Jerrimer sighed deeply, then rallied himself and made an effort to join in. "Even in elven lore we have no record," he informed them. "But our legends tell of unendurable servitude and an uprising of our people in bloody battle, before we made the long trek westwards into Irriyan."

"We dwarfs have a similar legend," said Diblin. "It is rumoured that we built our mountain halls for sanctuary after we had slain the tyrants who ruled us. 'Twas long ago but, in their games, our dwarflings still fear the giant's tread. And as a race, we have vowed never again to recognize one of our own breed, or any other breed, as master."

"Thus have we learnt our lesson," murmured Kadmon. "And so it is written in the edicts of Llandor: let us respect the life of all creatures that we neither dominate them nor allow ourselves to be dominated."

"I wish we could learn that where we come from," sighed Gwillym.

"Fat chance," muttered Roderick.

"To dominate, or to be dominated, is the basis of our society," said Carrie. "Men dominate women, women dominate children, bosses dominate at work."

"And religious leaders dominate congregations," said Gwillym.

"And western civilization dominates the rest of the world," said Roderick.

"If we don't dominate others in at least some respects, then we're considered to be failures," said Carrie.

"Sick, isn't it?" said Gwillym.

"Then be glad you are here," Kadmon told him.

"Maybe I am," said Gwillym.

"You mean you no longer want to go back to our world?" asked Carrie.

"Not any more," said Gwillym.

Carrie nodded.

"I don't think I do either," she said. "Even after all we've been through, there's something about Llandor..."

"A kind of freedom," said Roderick.

"Yes," said Carrie. "There aren't any pressures on us. It's only when I think about my mother..."

She paused, chewed on her lip, her silence more eloquent than words. She was beautiful, thought Roderick, despite her tattered trousers and goat-skin boots plastered with mud, her mouse-brown hair tangled and unkempt and the hungry hollows of her face. It was the kind of beauty that had nothing to do with looks, but sprang from something inside her, a strength or a softness, he was not sure which. He only knew she had changed, that he liked what she had become, the deep inner nature of a girl he had once thought he hated.

"What about you?" she asked him. "Do you want to stay here?"

"I *never* wanted to go back," admitted Roderick.

"No," said Carrie. "I can understand that. I don't suppose things were ever very nice for you, Rod."

She walked beside him, after that. They did not talk much, no more than she had talked to Kadmon the day before, or Roderick had talked with Diblin over all the previous days, but they were there for each other, companions in the same silence. And he had changed, too, things gone out of him to be replaced by other things, a kind of quietness, mostly, a sense of participation in everything around him.

He was open to the land and everyone who lived there – to Jerrimer's sadness, Diblin's pain and Kadmon's power – to the frost on the hills and the scudding shadows of clouds and the nearby song of a gorse chat. Somehow everything mattered, as nothing had ever mattered back in Ditchford, a myriad existences that he feared might end because he was there. It was as if his very presence threatened the order and constancy of things – Maeve dead because of him, Janine bitten by a boggart, Diblin injured—

"What are you thinking?" Carrie asked him.

"That we shouldn't stay in Llandor," Roderick sighed.

She looked at him in alarm.

"Just now you said you never wanted to go back."

"That doesn't make it right, though, does it?"

"I don't understand."

"Because of us Maeve and Festy..."

"Don't say that, Rod!"

"But it's true," Roderick persisted. "Up until now all we've been thinking about is our own safety. But if we were to think about..."

"They weren't bound to help us," muttered Carrie. "They weren't bound to come with us. We didn't force them and I don't want to think about it. Not just now."

"Sooner or later we'll have to," Roderick said.

She continued to walk beside him along the ruins of a road, but something was different. The silence between them seemed strained and fearful, and when she leant on the parapet of the bridge that crossed the River Crawdle she was not looking at the view, but gazing within at the darkness Roderick had created. Her expression was joyless, and her elven cloak reflected the stones and the sky.

"I'm sorry," he said.

"It's not your fault," she murmured.

"I wish I'd never mentioned..."

"Even if we wanted to go home, we couldn't," she said. "Doorways between worlds don't open very often. Gwillym's been waiting five years, remember? Wrong or right we're here to stay, Rod, so we may as well make the best of it. There's nowhere else we can go."

"There is one place—"

"No!" Carrie said sharply.

"If we're going to consider the others—"

"Things will be all right once we reach Seers' Keep."

"Maybe they will," agreed Roderick. "But it's the getting there that worries me, Carrie. What else is going to happen? What else am I going to end up killing?"

"It was necessary, Roderick."

"But that doesn't make it right, does it? Those boggarts were sentient beings and I killed them. And what other kinds of creatures are we going to be attacked by? How many others are going to die because they are with us? Diblin? Jerrimer?"

"Please, Rod!"

He heard the distress in her voice, but there was nothing he could say to end it, no way he could help. He leant on the parapet beside her, each of them locked in their separate silence. Frosted distances spread before them, the river winding silver through the gorge below, the marsh beyond it and the hills over which they had already travelled. If they cared about Llandor, cared about their companions, then they had no choice but to—

"There's got to be another way," said Carrie.

"Like what?" asked Roderick.

"I don't know. And we can't make a decision anyway, not without Craig. He's in it, too. So there's no point in us..."

She stopped as the others caught up with them, chewed at the chaps on her lips until they bled. And the eyes of the Black Mage raked their faces, and Gwillym posed the inevitable question.

"What's going on with you two then?"

"Nothing," Carrie said miserably.

"Just a slight difference of opinion," said Roderick.

"About what?" demanded Kadmon.

"Spit it out," growled Diblin. "We don't want a repeat of yesterday! People stomping off and abandoning the rest of us. We're all in this together, remember?"

"Roderick thinks we oughtn't to be," said Carrie.

"Does he indeed?" Kadmon murmured. "And who is he to think what ought to be? The mayhaps and might-be's and how each will affect the outcome of the future are for the Seers to unravel, perhaps, but not for us to know, else in our fear we may cast ourselves from the parapet of this bridge and end it all."

"That may be easier than living," Jerrimer said desperately.

"For a coward!" Diblin said harshly.

Kadmon turned his black gaze on Roderick.

"What we do is not for you," he said, "for you may well not be worth it. But for Llandor, for Irriyan, for Diblin's mountain halls, we all will die if we must. Remember that. Not for you do we make this journey. Not for you do we freeze and hunger in this place twixt nowhere and nowhere, but for our own satisfaction. And where we ought to be, for your information and had you not stayed us, is at the gateway to the Moor Wife's cottage."

His speech completed, Kadmon strode away.

"And that's telling you," said Gwillym.

"Partisans, all of us," muttered Jerrimer. "I wonder if Maeve knew that?"

"He's right about another thing," Diblin said gruffly. "I shall turn goblin and kill a rabbit if I don't soon get fed!"

Carrie laughed, and for her sake Roderick allowed himself to be persuaded that it was not his presence which threatened the security of the land, and not him the Grimthane was after. Why should he think, even for one minute, that he had that much significance when in the world he came from he had no significance at all?

But once on the moor itself, with the wind mourning around the ruined buildings above them, his sense of oppression grew. He felt gripped by an overwhelming sadness and the weather reflected his mood. Clouds snatching away the sun, piled grey upon grey over the high hills. And the ruins depressed him – all that remained of a race of giants – so what hope had he of survival? Even in Llandor his future seemed as bleak as it had been at home in Ditchford. Or maybe it was something to do with the season?

Everything dead and dying at the onset of winter.

Downhill, around the margins of Sedge Marsh, the osiers had lost their leaves. Frost paled the rushes, and fingers of ice spread along the channels of open water. No life anywhere besides themselves, and a flock of geese that came waddling to meet them. Necks outstretched and beaks agape, they cackled their welcome or warning.

"Grandmother Holly's goose-feather beds!" said Kadmon.

"Which means we have not far to go?" asked Jerrimer.

"They are not looking very friendly," said Gwillym.

Diblin brandished his crutch. "Boo!" roared the dwarf, and his leg gave way beneath him. Honking and cackling, the geese retreated as he lay spread-eagled on the frozen grass. And the first few flakes of snow began to fall, settling on his beard and hair and eyebrows like monstrous dandruff.

Carrie giggled.

"That was brave of you, Diblin!"

"You are saving us all from a good pecking," said Gwillym.

"At risk to life and limb," muttered Jerrimer.

"Do not mock the afflicted!" Kadmon said with false severity.

But they laughed anyway, even Jerrimer, wildly, hysterically as Roderick hauled Diblin to his feet and retrieved his crutch. And the dwarf limped on, scowling and annoyed, rejecting any further assistance, his tattered rat-skin trousers flapping in the now increasing wind.

They hastened on in Diblin's wake, only to stop beside him as they rounded the flank of the hill. Beyond a white picket fence was a garden in a valley, dark earth free of frost where the snow failed to settle. Roses, out of season, released their scents and ripening strawberries lined the path. Summer vegetables grew among the flowers, and further up the valley a thatched cottage snuggled in the lee of the hills. Rowan trees laden with scarlet berries seemed to guard it and the warm air wafting in Roderick's face reminded him of Woodholm.

"The Moor Wife's cottage," Kadmon announced.

"And a touch of elven magic," Jerrimer sighed.

"Isn't it wonderful?" breathed Carrie.

"So don't let's stand outside," said Gwillym. "Please to be stirring your stumps, Diblin, and open the gate."

The dwarf sniffed.

"There's a smell!" he said warily.

"Of roses," said Carrie.

"Or hot buttered toast," Jerrimer said

longingly.

"A reek of something foul," said Diblin.

"Goose droppings probably," said Gwillym.

"Or us in need of a bath?" said Roderick.

"Just get on in there, Diblin!" Carrie commanded.

But the dwarf stayed motionless, stubborn and suspicious, until Kadmon pushed past him and opened the gate. In a small procession, with Diblin bringing up the rear, they headed up the flagstone path. The snow, whirling about them, melted at a touch and the door opened before they could knock. A shrunken old woman with piercing blue eyes beckoned them inside.

"Grandmother Holly!" Kadmon said warmly.

"So we meet again," the old woman murmured. "How long has it been?"

"I measure my years in wrinkles, Wanderer. You in the miles you have travelled. And talk can wait. Take yourself in. There is food on the table, hot water for baths and feather beds awaiting."

Kadmon lowered his head and entered with a rustle of robes. And Carrie followed, meeting the Moor Wife's gaze, saying her name and accepting the blessing of the old woman's smile, before she crossed the threshold. Then it was Roderick's turn. Clawed hands clasped his own. Fathomless blue, the old eyes gripped and held him, and deep in his mind, just for a moment, he thought he heard her speak.

"Ah, so it's you, is it? You killed the boggarts. And not a scratch on you, not a trace of the Grimthane's venom. Immune, are you? Well, you will need to be, boy."

"I'm Roderick," he said aloud.

The old woman nodded.

"Away in with you, Roderick. And beware who you trust."

He wanted to ask her what she meant but she had already turned to Gwillym. "Gwillym the Mapper!" the Moor Wife said, as Roderick ducked below the doorway and entered her cottage.

He had grown used to the open air, vast spaces of land and the sky above his head, cold and quietness and slow starvation. So already the room seemed cramped and crowded, too many people in too small a space; the lamplight dim, the ceiling low, the fire unbearably hot and the table laden with too much food. Vegetable stew with parsley dumplings, plums and apples and strawberries, seed cake and scones, dishes of cream and butter and jam.

Carrie and Kadmon were already seated, Janine beside them wearing a white calico smock, her fair hair washed clean, long and gleaming in the lamplight. Roderick should have seen in her a greater beauty than he had seen in Carrie, but something spoilt her, the unwelcoming expression on her face, maybe, or the strange discontentment in her eyes. It was there in Craig, too, seated on a stool beside the fire, a kind of sourness that his voice belied.

"Hi, Rod. Come and meet Umla."

Roderick stared, but not at Craig. Someone sat beside him, someone small as a child, in a blue cotton dress, stirring the contents of a blackened saucepan. She had greyish skin and pointed ears and a tuft of hair tied with a red ribbon on the top of her head. Round milky-white eyes gazed curiously at Roderick, then widened in terror as Diblin came roaring in.

"A goblin!" howled the dwarf. "I said there was a stench of something foul!"

"Stop him!" wailed Carrie.

Umla shrieked as Diblin made to attack. Things from the table smashed on the floor, and the stool toppled as Craig and Kadmon lurched to their feet, but Roderick was quicker. He grabbed the crutch that would have smashed the goblin girl's skull, twisted it from Diblin's hands and stood his ground, an immovable obstacle between the dwarf and his intended victim. Outraged and thwarted, Diblin's clenched fist struck him in the stomach but then Gwillym and Jerrimer rushed to Roderick's aid, held the dwarf's arms and dragged him away, held him, kicking and howling in fury, until his rage abated.

The room grew still. The Moor Wife calmly closed the outer door. Kadmon re-seated himself, and the little goblin cowered at Roderick's side.

"No hurt Rod...no hurt Umla," she whimpered.

"He won't," Roderick assured her.

"We won't let him, see?" said Gwillym.

Craig replaced the poker in the hearth.

"Have you gone flaming mad, Diblin?"

"If mad are the thoughts then mad will be the deeds," the Moor Wife muttered. "Two last night and now another with venom a-festering in his heart and head."

"What do you mean by that?" Craig asked indignantly.

"She means us!" Janine said crossly.

"Never mind that!" Diblin shook himself free of his captors. Beads of sweat shone on his forehead. His beard bristled and his eyes were feverishly bright. "Since when have you given house-room to goblins, old woman?" he demanded.

"Since first Umla came to me," the Moor Wife replied.

"The barbaric blob of slime-spawn!"

"Must you hold her responsible for her parentage, dwarf?"

"She is as likely to take a lump from our throats as soon as look at us!"

"She is quite content with a diet of birds and

rabbits."

"Goblins are carnivores!" growled Diblin.

"That is indeed Umla's nature," the Moor Wife agreed.

"It was also Festy's nature," said Carrie.

"And there's nothing wrong with eating meat," said Craig. "We all do it where we come from. Ask Gwillym, ask Carrie and Roderick. It's in our nature, too."

"We have a choice!" Carrie said curtly.

"And when in Rome..." said Gwillym.

Craig took a fork, fished a lump of meat from the saucepan, and proceeded to eat it.

"It's good," he said. "Why don't you have some?"

"No, thank you," said Gwillym.

He seated himself at the table.

And Janine glared at Craig.

"Sometimes, you make me feel absolutely sick!" she said.

"Sick indeed," sighed the Moor Wife. "And worse than a boggart bite is the touch of the Grimthane on a mortal mind. Attend to your own ills, Keera's daughter. And sit down, all of you. Sit down and eat. You too, dwarf. Unless you would prefer to camp outside rather than share this roof with a goblin?"

Wearily, defeatedly, Diblin took his place at the old woman's table, Jerrimer beside him. Janine stared sullenly at her plate, and Carrie was marooned in her own silence. Even Gwillym seemed affected by something – moody and uncommunicative. And wrapped in his cloak of darkness the Black Mage crumbled a morsel of bread between lean fingers and brooded on his own thoughts. The tension was almost tangible. It was as if, from the moment they had stepped inside the Moor Wife's cottage, they had become gripped by a kind of a contagion that festered inside them, vestiges of violence and undercurrents of hate.

Something was happening, thought Roderick, something terrible was happening to all of them, everything ugly being heaved to the surface and destroying the friendship that had grown between them. He clutched his stomach where Diblin had punched him. It was not the physical pain that grieved him, it was the sudden inexplicable loss of whatever it was that had once united them, the upsurge of nastiness and Craig's disgusting demonstration of human nature.

Beware who you trust, the Moor Wife had said.

A hand tugged at Roderick's sleeve and he turned his head.

"You want?" murmured Umla.

Her pale eyes shone in the firelight, and her teeth gleamed white as she smiled. It was meat she offered him, too, a leg of rabbit on a fork, cooked with herbs and dripping with juices, a gesture of friendship or a gift, perhaps, all she had to give in return for his protection. And Craig smirked, wiped his mouth, and waited to see what he would do.

Roderick shook his head.

"No, thank you, Umla."

"Take it," said Craig.

"Is good," said Umla.

"She's right," said Craig. "Try it, Rod. You know you want to."

Roderick stared at him.

He was being offered a choice, not by Umla, but by Craig, and it had nothing to do with eating meat in a land where the practice was considered socially unacceptable. It was a question of taking sides, of aligning himself with Craig in some kind of confrontation. He was not sure about the issues. He only knew that the old order had broken down, that Craig was not who he had been, a prefect at Lydminster comprehensive school, someone important, in a position of authority, to whom Roderick was obliged to defer to and encouraged to emulate. Here, in Llandor, Craig had lost ground and lost face. He was no more special than Roderick was. But he wanted to be. With a piece of forbidden meat he tried to assert himself, and Roderick, if he accepted the same, would be accepting his leadership as well.

"No, thank you," he repeated. "I told you the other night...no animal or person is going to die because of me, not ever again."

He saw a flicker of sheer hate in Craig's eyes, a trace of hurt in Umla's. He wanted to tell her that it was not she he was rejecting, but instead he turned to meet the silence in the room behind him. They were all watching him, deadpan faces void of expression – except for the Moor Wife, smiling shrewdly, and the dark snake-like glitter of Kadmon's eyes beneath his hood. The Black Mage reached for an apple from the fruit bowl and tossed it casually in Roderick's direction.

"Try that," he instructed.

"Yes," said the Moor Wife. "You try that, my dear."

And once again Roderick was being asked to choose.

CHAPTER FOURTEEN

Beyond the bathroom where water boiled in the copper and the air was hot with steam was a flag-stoned passage with sleeping spaces on either side. They were hardly rooms, just curtained cubby-holes hollowed from the hillside with stone shelves containing feather mattresses and duvets, snug and inviting. But the day had many hours to go before it was over and Roderick resisted the temptation to sleep and forget. He towelled himself dry, slipped on the brown hessian robe and rope sandals Grandmother Holly had provided, and reluctantly returned to the living room.

Oil lamps flickered in the gloom of late afternoon. Chairs and the settle had been arranged in a wide half-circle round the fire, and everyone was seated, scrubbed clean, waiting for him to join them. Snow whirled whitely beyond the windows, the onset of winter falling thickly on the surrounding hills, softly covering the flowers and rowan trees in the garden. It was Roderick's last glimpse of the outside world before the Moor Wife drew the curtains against the coming night.

Umla smiled as he took his place on the empty stool beside her. The inevitable conference was about to begin. Strained faces surrounded him; Gwillym gaunt from the journey, Diblin glowering in the shadows by the chimney breast, his injured leg propped on a footstool and Jerrimer beside him, worn out from grieving. Craig and Janine seated together on the settle, and Carrie with them but not with them, holding herself apart. Only Kadmon, in his travel-stained robes, appeared unwearied by all they had been through and heedless of the tension in the room around him, the uneasy simmering of feelings that might yet explode.

And the Moor Wife rocked in her chair. She was hunched as a bird, her clawed hands gripping the arm rests, her shrewd eyes watching, unperturbed and aware of everything.

"And now, my dears, what are we to do with you?" she murmured.

"Must we be deciding that now?" sighed Gwillym.

"We have only recently arrived," objected Jerrimer.

"If you are to stay here..."

"Do we have any choice?" Craig asked sourly.

"There is always a choice," the Moor Wife replied.

"Not much of a one if the weather remains as it is," said Gwillym.

"We'll be cut off by the snow before long," said Carrie.

"We could be stuck here all winter," said Janine.

"At what risk to Umla and Grandmother Holly though?" asked Roderick.

"And at what risk to yourselves?" the old woman added. "These questions must be asked and answered, I fear."

"So who knows we're here?" asked Craig.

"No one," said Janine.

"Only the Wraiths," said Grandmother Holly.

"We timed our arrival during daylight," Kadmon protested.

"But Craig and Janine did not," the Moor Wife informed him. "It was well after dark before they entered my house, and we heard the wraiths a-crying, Umla and I."

"Is it important?" asked Janine.

"Dolts and dunderheads!" thundered Diblin. "Why else would we have come this way if not to avoid the Grimthane's watchers? All those days travelling over the dry hills wasted! We may as well have trumpeted our whereabouts to the world, or else returned to Droon and taken our chances!"

"We weren't to know!" snapped Craig.

"Mayhap no harm is done," Grandmother Holly said soothingly.

"Is everything that's not human in league with the Grimthane?" asked Carrie.

"Most things are for themselves and their own continuation," the Moor Wife said simply. "It is only when something threatens..." She paused, and glanced at Kadmon as if maybe she had said too much. Lamplight flickered in the depths of his eyes and, indifferently, he shrugged his shoulders.

"You mean us?" asked Carrie.

"So you've finally cottoned on," muttered Craig.

"I cottoned on long ago," said Carrie. "But I don't understand what threat we are to wraiths and kelpies and nixies. And what threat were Maeve and Festy?"

"None," Jerrimer said grimly. "None at all except that they were with you."

"So it's all our fault," Roderick said gloomily.

"No, it's not!" Janine said fiercely. "It is the Grimthane we are up against. The Fell One hunting us and preying on the fear of other things

– crows and boggarts and tree beings – using them for his own evil ends!"

"That being accepted," said Kadmon, "we must now decide what to do, and that decision concerns all of you, including Umla and Grandmother Holly."

"But obviously not you!" Craig said sarcastically.

"I'm here to advise," retorted Kadmon.

The room was warm from the fire and, on the table behind them, the oil lamp guttered, dimming the light so that nothing existed beyond the ring of their faces. As if in response the old woman rose, lit a candle on the mantelpiece and set it in the hearth. The small flame flickered, made a halo of light as Roderick watched it, and scented smoke, carried by a down draught, filled the air with a heady perfume.

Gwillym yawned.

"I know what I am wanting to do."

"Me too," muttered Janine.

"Sleep," said Carrie.

"For at least a week," said Gwillym.

"Or for a year," said Jerrimer.

"We're all too tired to carry on travelling," said Roderick.

Grandmother Holly nodded and smiled.

"Sleep," she murmured. "Sleep and healing. You are all in need of it, my dears, and it is one solution to our problems. The long sleep – the sleep of the hedgehog in a bed of leaves, the sleep of the dormouse in a nest of grasses – sleep, where the breath grows quiet, and thoughts are stilled, and the heartbeat is barely perceptible. Then the hunter may pass without knowing what lives we harbour here throughout the winter. This sleep I can offer you all, my dears, if in my hands you will place your trust."

There was a long silence.

The thought enticed, the old woman's words and the scent of the candle came stealing through Roderick's mind, soft and soporific. He had to struggle against it, fight to focus on what he really thought of the idea. It was a hideous suggestion, of course. Suspended animation...a kind of death. Uneasiness showed in Gwillym's eyes, and Carrie's face grew white as chalk.

"What are you saying?" she whispered.

"Hibernation," said Gwillym.

"Drug-induced, I suppose!" Craig said wrathfully.

"A concoction of certain herbs in certain proportions," the Moor Wife admitted. "'Tis nothing harmful, nothing to fear."

"You'll survive it well enough," Kadmon said curtly.

"My father did," said Janine. "When he came wounded into Irriyan the long sleep healed him and saved his life."

"It is used quite commonly in elven practice," said Jerrimer.

"Among dwarfs too," Kadmon said pointedly.

"The sleep of relief," murmured Jerrimer. "Dreamless and forgetting. No more hurt, no more pain, all fears and sorrows suspended. I have longed for it ever since Maeve..."

He had no need to say more. Among smoke and scent and candlelight, the same overwhelming longing was transferred to Roderick, lulling his fear. He wanted to sleep as much as Jerrimer did, and his eyelids felt heavy, about to succumb to a shared desire – until the dwarf's voice jerked him awake.

"That's as maybe!" growled Diblin. "But there is no way I shall be taking the long sleep, not with that treacherous dollop of toad-dump on the loose!"

"Umla not dollop!" the goblin girl said indignantly.

Grandmother Holly shook her head in protest, but her tone stayed soft and undisturbing.

"Umla's only treachery is to the Grimthane, dwarf."

"Goblins are servants of the Fell One, old woman!"

"Umla isn't," muttered Craig.

"What do you know about it, boy?"

"She escaped from Mordican – she told me that."

"Indeed she did," the Moor Wife confirmed.

Diblin sniffed.

In the Moor Wife's dressing gown and a pair of rabbit-fur slippers he was almost a comical figure. But heat from the fire and the residue of his former anger made him red in the face, and his beard bristled. He had always been tetchy and irascible, but this was sheer determined resistance, a confrontation that again involved them all. The candle-smoke shifted, stirred with sweetness, as Diblin waved a dismissive hand.

"If you were as wise as the rumours would have you, old woman, you would not be fooled by any tale that lying faggot-brained little floozy—"

Kadmon rose from his seat.

"Show him!" he snapped. "And let's get this over with!"

"If Umla is willing," the Moor Wife murmured.

The goblin girl clutched herself.

"No show!" she said. "No show nasty dwarf!"

"She has *you* labelled correctly," murmured Jerrimer.

Diblin's fierce eyes flashed with renewed ire. And there was a difference, thought Roderick, between the dwarf's fear of the long sleep and his own. All that lay between Diblin's acceptance of hibernation was the goblin girl's presence, an irrational hatred which could yet be swayed by common sense. But his own fear sprang from a lack of trust.

"Show me, Umla," said Janine.

At her request the goblin girl complied, unbuttoned the back of her frock and pulled down the sleeves enough for them to see. Shock showed in their eyes and on their faces. Her grey skin was covered with scars, as if she had been flayed repeatedly.

"Me whipped," she announced.

"Poor Umla," murmured Carrie.

"That's absolutely barbaric!" said Craig in disgust.

"It's how we used to treat slaves once," said Roderick.

"But no one in Llandor would do a thing like that!" said Janine.

"Not even you, Diblin," said Jerrimer.

"So who did it to you, Umla?" asked Gwillym.

"Nasty men and nasty goblins," said Umla.

Grandmother Holly explained. Umla had worked as a scullion in Mordican, in a palace in Asgaroth, the infernal city. She had been a slave to her master, as all creatures were who served the Grimthane or his minions. Her crime was to drop a plate of fruit, one of a set that could not be replaced. For that she had been beaten and sold, sent to work in a quarry hauling baskets of stone from dawn until dusk, and beaten again whenever she failed to keep pace.

"She ran away," the Moor Wife said. "Crossed the mountains last summer and found herself here with me – and more dead than alive she was when I took her in."

"Me hate," said Umla. "Me hate Mordican. Me hate the Grimthane and all what works with him. Me hate, see?"

The Black Mage stepped forward into the ring of light.

"And there you have it, dwarf! Now you have heard the Moor Wife's testimony, and heard the girl speak, will you not reconsider the prejudice of your breed and accept that one goblin soul, at least, is not beyond redemption?"

"You will not sleep easy unless you do," said Jerrimer.

"Maybe I'll sleep elsewhere!" muttered Diblin.

"Where?" asked Jerrimer.

"There are farms and villages around the edges of the moors!" Diblin said defiantly.

Carrie leant forward.

"But you can't go wandering the hills in weather like this, Diblin! You can't possibly, not with that leg of yours."

"You need to rest it," said Gwillym. "Give it time to heal, see?"

"And Umla will not harm you," Janine assured him.

"No more than she would harm the rest of us,"

said Jerrimer. "So if we are prepared to trust her, why can't you?"

"She's still a goblin," growled Diblin.

"And a goblin she will always be, for all she has tempered her nature," the Moor Wife agreed. "But more reason has she than you to loathe the Grimthane, dwarf. If there is a will to treachery among this company, it does not come from little Umla."

It was an odd thing to say, thought Roderick, almost an accusation. Why should any of them think of treachery? The Grimthane was an enemy of them all. They were on the run because of him, facing the long sleep because of him, and Benna, Festy and Maeve had died because of him. Yet Craig nodded, as if he gleaned a meaning from the Moor Wife's words and knew what she meant. Roderick's fear returned. If he were to trust and take the long sleep, would someone among them move to induce his death? Remove the threat of him, and Craig, and Carrie, from Llandor? The Moor Wife herself, perhaps? Or Kadmon?

"We are waiting, Diblin," the Black Mage announced.

"It's only your stiff-necked pride that's stopping you!" Janine said crossly.

"We need your acquiescence, dwarf," murmured Grandmother Holly.

"And if you will, I will," said Gwillym.

Diblin rose from his chair.

"Enough," he growled. "I've heard enough! I'll go along with you! I'll accept your opinion on the matter! I don't want to hear another word on the subject! Not one! And if we wake up wraiths when the sap rises, then don't anyone say I didn't warn them!"

He re-seated himself abruptly, and the tension in the room changed direction.

"Wraiths?" said Carrie. "Is that what we become if we die?"

"There will be no deaths!" Kadmon said impatiently. "No deaths, Carrie. Do you hear?"

She nodded and the atmosphere changed with her acceptance, relaxed and grew still. Janine and Gwillym smiled at each other and Jerrimer placed a friendly hand on the dwarf's shoulder. For them the issue was settled. They would surrender their bodies and minds into Grandmother Holly's keeping, and sleep unknowingly until whenever. In warmth and firelight, and the mind-numbing scent of the candle, the old woman's eyes shone blue and bright with triumph. But for Roderick the fear remained, and for Craig too, fear of the long sleep and the one unanswered question. The resistance Diblin had begun was yet to continue.

"How about you, my dears?" asked Grandmother Holly.

Craig shook his head.

"No way!" he retorted.

"He's scared," said Carrie.

"He's not the only one," said Roderick.

"How can you fear sleep?" asked Jerrimer.

"You are not reluctant to sleep at night," said Janine.

"It's not that kind of sleep," said Roderick. "It's like facing a general anaesthetic. Once you're unconscious you don't know what's going to happen to you or if you'll survive."

"But of course you will survive," the Moor Wife assured him.

"Sleep is sleep," said Jerrimer.

"You just sleep longer and deeper than usual," said Janine.

"Sleep good," said Umla.

"Good for whom?" Craig asked bitterly.

"For us," said Janine. "We're tired, Craig. I am, you are, everyone is. We need all the rest we can get before we tackle the next leg of our journey. And the wraiths know we're here. If they know, then other things might learn of our whereabouts, too. But if we can fool them into thinking we've left ... if our body functions are negligible and they can perceive no trace of us...It's our fault they know, Craig! Yours and mine! You have to go along with this, don't you see? It's the only chance we have of making things right again!"

"You just don't see it, do you?" Craig asked

angrily. "After all we talked about yesterday you still don't see it! You haven't got a clue what all this is really about!"

"So what is it about?" Kadmon asked quietly.

"You should know!" Craig retorted.

"Should I indeed?" Within the circle of light the darkness that was Kadmon prowled along the space of the mat, his black robes stirring the scent of the candle, its small flame reflecting in the glittering depths of his eyes. "I know your fear and know your mistrust," he murmured. "I know the source of it within your mind. The rest I may only guess. Is it fear of death, perhaps, as it was with Carrie? But death can strike at any time, waking or sleeping, so it cannot be death you fear or the long sleep itself. Something akin to death, maybe, or worse than it? The act of surrender, Craig, the fear of entrusting yourself into Grandmother Holly's keeping? And why should that trouble you, I wonder?"

Craig shrugged, and Roderick tried to think. Could he apply Kadmon's reasoning to himself? Was his fear of the same origin as Craig's? No, he thought. He, Roderick, had no reason not to trust the Moor Wife and no reason not to trust the long sleep. He would sleep and when he awoke he would still be himself as he was now – refreshed, perhaps, but essentially unchanged – with nothing lost but a few months of time. Was that what he feared? The gap in his life? Being deprived of the right to experience his own existence? That in itself was a kind of death, the loss of himself, a temporary passing into nothingness. But it was no worse than the nothingness he surrendered to nightly and if it served a purpose, if it ensured his own safety and the safety of everyone else, then he had no reason to resist.

"I'm willing," Roderick said bravely.

The old woman smiled at him.

"Umla and I will take good care of you," she promised.

"Idiot!" hissed Craig. "Can't you see what they're doing?"

"No," said Roderick.

"You always were thick, of course!"

Roderick shrugged and Craig leapt from his seat, picked up the candle and threw it in the fire. Flames spat and hissed as he turned back to face Roderick. The cloying scent began to clear and Craig's fists were clenched and his voice was wild.

"Think! Fight it! Use your brains – what few you have! You can't give in, Rod! You can't! It's what they want, what they're aiming for! Don't you see? If you give in now you're playing into their hands!"

"Whose hands?" asked Roderick in alarm.

"Theirs!" said Craig. "Theirs or the Grimthane's...it doesn't matter which. They're all the same as far as we're concerned! They all want the same thing!"

"What are you saying?" asked Carrie.

"I'm saying," said Craig through gritted teeth, "that there are certain people in this room who would like to eradicate various pieces of information that we happen to be carrying in our heads. And what better way is there of making us forget than doping us up to the eyeballs?"

The room fell silent. Eyebrows were raised, glances exchanged. He was talking of treachery, just as Grandmother Holly had, and naming no names. In her chair the Moor Wife rocked and smiled and in the dark beyond the firelight Kadmon perched on the edge of the table. His hood was thrown back, his hawk nose and the sweeping sleeves of his cloak gave him the look of a bird of prey, and his black eyes glittered. Roderick glanced at him nervously. The Black Mage was dangerous and always had been. He would kill if he had to, or wipe clean their minds in a blast of blue fire. But if that were his intention, he would have done so already. And what information did Craig or Roderick possess that could pose a threat to him?

"I still don't understand what you're talking about," said Carrie.

"I think he means hard roads and hamburgers," Janine said uneasily.

"Hamburgers?" said Jerrimer.

"What are hamburgers?" asked Diblin.

"Buns with meat in the middle," said Gwillym.

"So what have hamburgers got to do with it?" asked Roderick.

"Nothing!" Craig said harshly. "Nothing at all apart from what they represent! Human progress and a way of life! They don't want it here! They don't want any of it!"

Again the room fell silent, the faces of all within it – save Craig – showing puzzlement.

And Roderick frowned, unable to follow.

"They don't want what?" he asked.

"You're even thicker than I thought, Burden!" Craig said scathingly. "But even you must have learnt something at school! Basic radio systems, for example? A basic electrical circuit? How to refine petroleum from crude oil? Simple physics and simple chemistry, remember? Harness the steam from a kettle in an enclosed system, add escape valves and pistons, and the resulting energy will drive the wheel that will drive the machine, right? Or take a measure of saltpetre, add a measure of sulphur and a measure of carbon, and the result is gunpowder, right? If we put what we know into practical use, things are going to change, aren't they? Llandor will no longer be as it is, right? Now do you get it?"

Roderick stared at him. "*That's* why we're

being hunted?"

"What other reason can there be?"

"Because of what we are?" suggested Roderick.

"Evil," said Carrie.

"But we're not," said Craig. "We're not evil, are we? We're no more evil than anyone else."

Roderick shook his head.

"Even if you're right you surely can't suspect— ?"

"That is absurd, Craig!" Jerrimer said wearily.

"Have we come all this way and worked to keep you alive only to be accused of treachery?" growled Diblin.

"He doesn't mean you," Janine said miserably.

"Then who does he mean?" asked Gwillym.

Janine glanced at Kadmon and the Moor Wife. And Carrie laughed.

"You've got to be crazy, Craig!"

Craig stood alone before the fire, his fists still clenched, his face unseeable in the darkness, a one-time prefect at Lydminster comprehensive school, his brilliant future destroyed. He could not accept, could not see, that here in Llandor he was no longer important, that to Kadmon the Wanderer, and the old woman in her rocking chair, the sum total of all he knew amounted to almost nothing.

And even if Craig's suspicions were true, why should Roderick care if he woke up forgetting how to harness steam or make explosives? It was knowledge such as that that had created the world he had left behind, a world of wars and abattoirs, winners and losers and unfair competition, the world of a fat boy who had nothing going for him and nothing to hope for, to which he never wanted to return. He rose to his feet.

"I'm going to bed," he said simply.

CHAPTER FIFTEEN

"I'm going to bed," said Roderick.

Carrie understood.

It had nothing to do with surrender. It was a statement of trust, trust of Kadmon and Grandmother Holly and his own knowing, and a rejection of all Craig had said. Self-assured, as he had never been in their former world, Roderick took the lead and challenged the rest of them to follow his example. Firelight flickered on the ring of their faces. Kadmon waited and the Moor Wife rocked in her chair, both accused of treachery and denying nothing.

There was no point in them denying it, thought Carrie. Whatever they said, whether they lied or told the truth, Craig would not believe them.

Trust was more than a mental decision or a matter of intellectual reasoning. It sprang from somewhere else, from another level of being, from a non-reasoning part of oneself that counted for little or nothing in the world where she and Craig had come from. There everything had to be provable. But in Llandor, for good or ill, most things were taken on trust – and that included people. And somehow Carrie knew, as surely as Roderick knew, that there was no ill intent either in Kadmon or Grandmother Holly. But she could not say how she knew or convey that certainty to Craig. She could only do as Roderick did, accept the long sleep with no explanation – but Diblin beat her to it.

The crotchety dwarf leant on his crutch and heaved himself from his seat. "I've heard enough madness for one night," he declared. "Including my own. Brew your brew, old woman, I for one am ready to lay myself down."

"Me too," said Jerrimer.

"Sleep well," Kadmon said softly.

The Moor Wife nodded and rose from her chair, beckoned to Umla and hobbled from the room with Diblin and Jerrimer behind her. Unexpected tears hovered in Carrie's eyes. It was the first parting, the first intimation of loss, although Umla returned a moment later with logs for the fire and a blackened kettle which she set to boil. Her pale eyes shone and her white teeth gleamed as she smiled.

"You no come?" she said to Carrie.

"Not yet," Carrie replied.

She went away, a goblin girl dancing towards the glow of lantern light that shone through the kitchen door. Fresh herbs being pounded in a mortar smelt bitter-sweet and strong. And the sleeping berths waited, little curtained alcoves beneath the hill offering an end to everything.

"Anyone else?" asked Roderick, who had not yet gone.

Carrie hesitated. She was no longer afraid of the long sleep, but could not feel eager to begin it. There was still too much to be settled, and too much sadness in the moment of acceptance. It meant saying goodbye to everyone and not knowing when they would meet again or when she would see them. But Janine rose from the settle.

"I see no point in delaying," she declared.

"Providing you're sure," said Roderick.

"Which I am," said Janine.

"Turncoat!" hissed Craig.

"What does that mean?"

"I think he accuses you of treachery too," said Gwillym.

Her blue eyes looked puzzled.

"But why?" she asked. "Because I do not share his fear of the long sleep?" She turned to Craig.

"That has nothing to do with treachery!" she told him. "I am not against you, Craig. You may be right about some things, but there is one difference between the Grimthane and Grandmother Holly – he would likely do as you fear, but she would not."

"That's what you say!" Craig retorted.

Janine stared at him.

"Your knowledge will be intact when you awaken, I can assure you of that."

"Except that you can't," said Carrie.

"Can't what?" asked Janine.

"You can't assure him of anything."

"It's all right for you lot!" Craig said savagely. "Comparatively you've got nothing to lose! And what you get to drink might not be what I get to drink. And it's not just the Moor Wife anyway!"

"There is no answer to that," sighed Gwillym. "It is personal, see? We can all be knowing someone is wrong but we cannot be convincing them. Where we come from it is happening all the time. All manner of things are wrong, and we are most of us knowing it, but still they continue. No amount of reasoning will cause the surrender of another person's point of view, nor legislation either, nor even force. In our world they are fighting wars over differences of opinion."

Janine frowned.

"So he will be putting us all in danger because

of his stupidness and there is nothing we can do about it?"

"You wouldn't have said that yesterday!" snapped Craig. "Yesterday you were on my side!"

Janine stamped her foot impatiently.

"I'm not talking about sides! I'm talking about the long sleep!"

"And you are wasting your breath," murmured Kadmon. "Who sees a devil in disguise cannot see the raven. Craig will learn in time, but not through any words of yours or mine. Best go your way, Janine, and leave him be."

"In other words, bog off if that's what you want!" said Craig.

"Come on," Roderick urged gently.

The elf-girl shrugged.

Her voice sounded sad, and she no longer looked at Craig.

"I will bid you good night then."

"Yes," said Carrie. "Good night, Janine."

"Aren't you coming?" asked Roderick.

For Carrie it was the final challenge, but once again she hesitated. She could not have said why she wished to linger – a remnant of loyalty towards Craig, perhaps? A stubborn refusal to give up on him? Maybe she felt that if she turned her back on him now it would indeed be a form of treachery, the same kind of treachery she had exercised at Woodholm when she had walked out on the person Roderick had been. She shook her head.

"I'll stay," she said, "just for a while."

He nodded and trusted even her.

"I'll see you in the spring," he said.

"Yes," she said firmly.

When Roderick and Janine left, the room seemed empty. Voices and laughter could be heard in the kitchen, and shadows moved among the light, but Carrie was cut off from them, left behind and separated by her own choice from those who were her friends. The wind whined eerily round the eaves of the cottage and she had a feeling of lateness, of time running out, as if soon she must go whether Craig would or not.

She glanced towards him. He was glowering and belligerent, squatting on the stool Umla had vacated, staring at the fire and resenting everything that had happened. The blackened kettle steamed and sang. With valves and pistons it would drive a wheel that would drive a machine. But who wanted machines in Llandor? Who, apart from Craig, wanted hard roads and hamburger joints and gunpowder? Human beings had already ruined one world, so why should they be allowed to ruin this one? It was best as it was, its moors and marshes and forests unspoilt and untouched. But Craig could only compare and despise.

Almost unnoticed, the Black Mage moved to sit

in the Moor Wife's rocking chair, his legs outstretched, his dark eyes glinting in the firelight. At best he was a harbinger of disaster, Janine had said, and at worst he was a servant of the Grimthane. But for all she was in awe of him, Carrie could not believe him evil. He had saved her life, dragged her from the depths of Sedge Marsh, done his utmost to heal Janine's arm and Diblin's leg. And walking beside him over the dry hills she had felt secure in his presence, as if he protected her and protected them all.

But Craig did not think like that, did not believe it, and there was nothing she or anyone else could say that would sway him. It had to be some kind of demonstration, she thought. And at the moment she thought it, Kadmon moved.

She held her breath as the Black Mage leant forward, took a pinch of powder from the pouch at his belt and flung it on the fire. Craig yelped and drew back as the flames roared upwards, fizzed blue and green and purple, and exploded with a shower of sparks. The kettle tipped, hissed and steamed as Gwillym righted it, and acrid smoke drifted around the room.

"We already have gunpowder," Kadmon said quietly.

Craig gaped at him.

"And what else were you offering?" Kadmon asked smoothly. "Petroleum refinement? Steam turbines? Hydro-electricity? We have the know-how for those things as well."

"I've seen no evidence!" Craig said hotly.

"It is true, nevertheless," murmured Gwillym. "Potentially, by utilising the torrent streams of the Kelsfell, the Seers could provide lighting and heating for the whole of the central area of Llandor. Potentially they could mass-produce steel and refine petroleum—"

"So why don't they?" Craig demanded.

Gwillym spread his hands.

"I am not party to their full deliberations," he said. "But it is not the principle of industrial and technological advancement that is being objected to, it is the possible effects of it, see?"

"No, I don't see!" Craig said angrily.

"If you were to think about the morality of its application..."

"What the hell are you talking about, Gwillym? People here are living in the Dark Ages! If the Seers know about technology then why isn't it being used?"

"And how would you have us use it?" Kadmon asked quietly. "Indiscriminately, as you have done in your world? Should we enslave the dwarven race and set them to mine coal for us in ever-increasing quantities? Introduce steel production in every major town and disregard the blacksmith's trade? Replace feet with wheels?

Hands with machines? Breastfeeding with baby-milk formulas? Art and craft with mass-production? The power of individuals to manage their own lives with the enforced prison system of factories and offices? We know of your world, Craig. We know how it works. We learn a little more each time a doorway opens and another person enters. It is not what we wish for Llandor."

Craig sat silently for a moment, then he nodded. His face twisted and his voice was laden with scorn.

"You suppress it, don't you?" he said.

"Suppress what?" asked Kadmon.

"Knowledge!"

"No," Kadmon said smoothly. "Knowledge is the responsibility of the knower. It is up to whoever possesses it to decide what to do with it – whether or not it should be applied or shared. We can advise, that is all. And that is the purpose of Seers' Keep and why we are taking you there."

"We are immigrants, see?" said Gwillym. "We are all arriving here without a passport and with no one to vouch for us. Understandable, isn't it, that we should be up for question?"

"And should you fall into the Grimthane's hands, he will do more than question," Kadmon said darkly. "His thirst for knowledge is untempered by any moral consideration. For that reason you are right to fear both me and the Moor Wife. Were we to think the Fell One might succeed in his quest, and what you know be given over to him, then we would be bound to take precautions. And yes, we would wipe clean your mind if we knew how. As it is, if the occasion arises, we must content ourselves with slitting your throat instead."

Craig swallowed.

His face had paled as Kadmon spoke.

But Carrie laughed.

"You wouldn't do that," she said.

"Would I not?" asked Kadmon.

"No," said Carrie. "Neither you nor Grandmother Holly, because you would have done it already. To be on the safe side you would have got rid of all of us – me and Roderick as well, and Gwillym, too, probably. Killing people might be the Grimthane's way but isn't yours, Kadmon. You'd only kill to save Llandor, or to save us."

"Except when the two conflict," muttered Craig.

Carrie turned to him.

"But they don't," she said earnestly. "Don't you see? You're not that important, Craig, and what you know isn't that important. I mean, you don't know any more than Gwillym knew when he came here – well, a bit, perhaps, but not much, none of us do. And we know a damned sight less than Kadmon, or Keera, or Grandmother Holly. We're no match for the wisdom of the Seers, Craig. They don't need what we know. We only matter because the Grimthane is after us. And it's the Grimthane we have to fear, not Kadmon or Grandmother Holly. They're only trying to help us, shield us, take us to a place of safety. That's all any of them have been doing – Kern and Keera, Janine and Jerrimer and Diblin. Don't you see that?"

Craig stared at the fire, stubborn, unconvinced, accepting nothing. Outside in the darkness the wind increased in strength, rattled the window panes and the leaves of the rowan trees beyond the cottage door. For a moment Carrie thought she heard unearthly voices wailing in the distance, but the sound of them was lost in the wildness of the storm, the crank of the pump in the washroom, the Moor Wife's steps along the passage and the waste of Carrie's own breath.

There was no point in talking. She knew, by her own experience, how hard it was to admit you had been wrong. It was having to let go of all your thoughts and feelings and judgements, everything that made you what you were. And it could change everything – change how you saw people and change yourself. I was wrong, Roderick, was all Carrie had said. And then, gradually, she had stopped hating and begun to love; the land she had walked through and the people she had met –

Maeve and Jerrimer, Kadmon and the Moor Wife, even a bad-tempered dwarf by the name of Diblin. But Craig still clung to their former world, the same thoughts and opinions he had always had; afraid to let go of them, afraid of what he would be without them, afraid even to sleep in case he changed and forgot.

"Even if you do forget," she said, "it's not irretrievable, is it? Because it's still there. Everything we learnt is back at Woodholm – three school bags full of homework books – which is more than you're ever likely to remember, Craig."

"Books?" said Kadmon.

Carrie turned her head.

"Our school homework books," she told him. "Chemistry and physics, I think it was. I don't know what Roderick had because he was in a different grade. But they're all there at Woodholm. Keera's looking after them for us."

"Does she know what she guards?" asked Kadmon.

"I doubt it," said Gwillym. "Her only concern was to ensure the safety of Craig, Carrie and Roderick."

"Which we have done," said Kadmon, "in spite of what Craig may think. Here with the Moor Wife no harm is likely to befall them." The rocking chair clattered as he rose to his feet. "I'll be on my way," he said.

"You're not leaving?" asked Carrie.

"I am not named Wanderer for nothing," Kadmon replied. "It is not in my nature to remain in one place for long and you, for now, have no further need of me. I will go to Woodholm, retrieve those books of yours and take them to Seers' Keep. Go and ask the Moor Wife for provisions, Gwillym. Ask, too, if she has a cloak of wool or fur for protection against the weather."

Gwillym nodded and left the room.

And restlessly the Black Mage prowled the carpet.

"What if the Grimthane has already visited Woodholm?" Carrie asked fearfully. "What if he's already found our books?"

"Keera would not relinquish them," Kadmon said.

Carrie's voice rose. "But if he went there with a whole army of goblins she wouldn't have had any choice, would she? They could be dead, both of them, Kern and Keera! And how can we possibly stay here and sleep without knowing?"

"If Llandor had a telephone network we could ring up and find out," muttered Craig.

"Poles and cables!" Kadmon said scathingly. "What need have we of those? We have scryers a-plenty and the ether sings with each identity. If Keera ceased to be, the whole of Llandor would know, the loss of her felt in every living heart."

Carrie wanted to believe him, but coming from a world where no one, apart from the famous, seemed to matter – where millions died each day in wars and droughts and famines – the very idea seemed incredible. Were people really so important here? Did each one matter so much that their death or absence would be noticed by everyone else, the loss of them carried by the air and Llandor incomplete without them? Did she and Craig and Roderick matter like that? Was that why everyone cared so much and was willing to help them? Because they were here? Living souls in a living land and inextricably a part of it?

Suddenly, she did believe it. In Kadmon's words she realized her own worth. Tears filled her eyes, an overwhelming humility, a sense of belonging. It was as if she had been born in the wrong place, in the wrong world and now, finally, she had come home. She gazed at the fire in the waiting silence. And she wanted to thank Kadmon, for the meaning he had just bestowed upon her and for saving her life. But other voices intruded. Draped in sheets and blankets, Janine and Roderick and Jerrimer had left their sleeping berths and come to bid him goodbye.

"You are going then, Kadmon?"

"Leaving us and returning to Woodholm?"

"Will you be coming back?"

"Will you be here when we wake?"

"Travelling with us for the remainder of our journey?"

Kadmon spread his hands.

"Who knows?" he said. "Paths cross and for a while we travel together, but nothing is for ever. Circumstances change and we go our separate ways and who knows when we are destined to meet again this side of our graves? Mayhap we will. It is my intention to return, but Fate may have other intentions. Who knows?"

Jerrimer nodded.

"In that case we should thank you," he said.

"For what?" asked Kadmon.

"For a cairn of stones," said Jerrimer.

"And for healing my arm," said Janine.

"And Diblin's leg," said Roderick.

"And for leading us here," said Carrie. "And for saving my life."

The Black Mage smiled.

"Live long and gladly," he replied.

Then his time with them was almost over. Gwillym returned with a backpack, the Moor Wife hobbling behind him and Umla with her arms full of fur. It was a rabbit-skin cape she carried, long and hooded. She had made it herself from the consequences of her nature, each skin carefully stretched and dried and sewn together. It was all she possessed and all she could give – goblin charity presented with a laugh and likewise acknowledged. Over his robes the Black Mage donned it, accepted the backpack, and picked up his staff that stood beside the door.

"Travel safely," the Moor Wife said.

"And you guard them well, old woman."

"Umla guard too," the goblin girl told him.

Satisfied, Kadmon nodded, but then his dark gaze rested on Craig who sat brooding by the fire, a non-participant determinedly ignoring him. The question of Craig remained, the only issue that had yet to be settled. Carrie saw the laughter twinkle in the black depths of Kadmon's eyes, and he glanced at the Moor Wife as if for permission. Then, at a nod of her head, he acted; drew another handful of dust from the pouch at his belt and once again cast it into the flames.

It was not gunpowder this time, although Craig instinctively yelped and withdrew. A billow of white smoke obscured the apple logs burning and thickened to a cloud. Images shimmered within it as Carrie stared. Behind her the door opened with a gust of cold and darkness. She heard the shriek of wind sweeping down from the heights of Harrowing Moor and an eerie wailing of voices that suddenly ceased as the door closed again. Kadmon had departed, the saddest parting of all for Carrie. Brief tears shimmered in her eyes, but no one saw. All their attention was fastened on the vision he had left behind – a causeway leading through a turquoise sea to an island hung with light.

"Seers' Keep," murmured Gwillym.

"Seers' Keep indeed," agreed the Moor Wife.

Carrie dashed a hand across her eyes. And the island drifted closer as she watched. It reminded her of St Michael's Mount but with a difference. It had a dreamlike quality, was more beautiful, more magical than any place on Earth. The buildings were almost translucent; white walls shot with glassy colours and gilded towers, colonnades and balconies that were hung with flowering creepers, soaring archways leading from flighted streets into shady courtyards with lily pools and fountains, walled gardens and grassy spaces, trees wherever trees would grow and flowers everywhere. Carrie had never seen so many flowers, rich hot blooms spilling from tubs and window boxes and hanging baskets, and flowers of the shadows in shades of blue and cream and lavender, and all the variegated depths of evergreen.

A fairy tale city seemed to surround her – or else she floated through it – her physical body insubstantial as air. She felt the sun on her face, the soft sea breeze in her hair, glimpsed through arched windows a quiet library filled with books, a shadowy scriptorium where elven scribes worked on illuminated pages, a circular hall tiled with magical symbols. People wearing white robes moved through a laboratory full of chemical apparatus, others crossed a quadrangle – students, maybe, with their arms full of books; dwarfs and elves and humans. She heard snatches of their laughter and a drift of music.

Then, on the balcony of a high tower, a woman stood staring out to sea. Her black hair moved in the wind and her face was timeless, her eyes green as moss, smiling across the distances as if she saw. But the vision of her faded as the cloud of Kadmon's magic slowly dispersed. The wash of the sea on the island shores was replaced by the hiss of flames from the fire, the white blazing light by the room's darkness, the woman's face by the Moor Wife's wrinkled countenance. Only the memory remained, the memory of her eyes, her smile, casting a spell on Carrie's mind.

"Who was she?" whispered Craig.

"Merganna," the old woman murmured. "Her name is Merganna."

"Merganna the Enchantress," said Jerrimer.

"That, too, for some," agreed the Moor Wife. "She was at Seers' Keep when I was there those untold years ago. We were young together, Merganna and I. And she is young still, preserved by her magic, no doubt."

"My mother has told me of her," said Janine.

"She's very beautiful," said Roderick.

"More beautiful still when you meet her," said Gwillym.

"Maybe I will," mused Jerrimer.

"And that's where we're going?" asked Craig.

The Moor Wife's blue eyes twinkled in the firelight.

"Indeed you are," she assured him. "To Seers' Keep and the Lady Merganna, where all knowledge, all wisdom is gathered. And the sooner you take the long sleep the sooner you will be there. Time is no time when you are not aware of it. Or do you prefer to be conscious throughout the winter and caged in this cottage with Umla and me?"

"No," said Craig.

And Carrie laughed.

"You've changed your mind!" she said.

"What's wrong with that?" asked Craig.

"Nothing," said Gwillym. "Nothing at all."

"And now can we go to bed?" asked Roderick, from the door.